RITUALS
OF SURGERY

BY RICHARD SELZER

RITUALS OF SURGERY

MORTAL LESSONS: NOTES ON THE
ART OF SURGERY

CONFESSIONS OF A KNIFE

LETTERS TO A YOUNG DOCTOR

TAKING THE WORLD IN FOR
REPAIRS

RITUALS
OF SURGERY

BY RICHARD SELZER

Quill

WILLIAM MORROW

New York

The following short stories have appeared previously in
other publications: "Museum Piece" and "Little Saint
Hugh," *Antaeus*; "Train Ride," *Esquire*; "Fairview," *New
American Review*; "The Fur Baby," *Playgirl*; "The
Harbinger," *Harper's* magazine.

Published originally by Harper's Magazine Press in
association with Harper & Row Publishers, Inc.

Library of Congress Cataloging-in-Publication Data

Selzer, Richard.
Rituals of surgery.

I. Title.
PS3569.E585R57   1987   813'.54   86-30473
ISBN 0-688-06490-6 (pbk.)

Printed in the United States of America

First Quill Edition

1 2 3 4 5 6 7 8 9 10

To Janet

Contents

RITUALS
OF SURGERY

Museum Piece

An interesting journal lies where I placed it, at the bottom of a pile of manuscripts in the Historical Room of the Museum of the Royal College of Surgeons. I shall list others of the memorabilia in the room because I feel that it is important to see objects as well as ideas in their context, and that something is lost when things are torn from their beds and held up naked to the eye. Let us hurry past the cases of raspatories, uvulotomes, and other old surgical instruments, although some of these are quite charming, I assure you. Also we must not dally near the collection of etuis and other surgeons' cases, even number 14, which is covered in green shagreen ornamented with tortoise shell and silver, and which belonged to Baron Dimsdale, who at the desire of the Empress Catherine in 1768 traveled to Saint Petersburg to inoculate her young son against smallpox. I placed the journal here out of a sense of the rightness of things.

Here is an abbreviated list of my favorites. May the others forgive me!

Two silver porringers, each with four legs, which stand on the floor to receive blood during letting. One is embossed with a scene of Diana spearing a hind; the other shows a fresco of lewd Ceylonese acrobats. (Fresh warm blood streaming onto polished silver!)

A coconut shell used for the same purpose in barbarous places.

3

Benjamin Bell's harelip pins and forceps, and an elaborate mouth gag.

Latta's eyelid retractor, a little broad hook for keeping down the underlid when the eye is to be fixed by the hasta, a needle mounted on a handle.

Japanese gold wire needles for acupuncture.

A pewter enema-syringe for self-use, which belonged to P. J. deLoutherbourg, R.A., a well-known artist of the eighteenth century, who turned quack doctor and lived at Chiswick (1740–1812).

The fenestrated Mains de Fer and cephalotribes for crushing the skulls of infants with heads too large for delivery. (I have the classic one by Assalini and the less modish of Baudelocque.)

Numbers 100 and 101 are cauls, used as charms against drowning.

The heart of a calf into which are inserted pins, thorns, and twigs of witch hazel, to be used to the injury of one's enemies. (This one, incidentally, was found in 1902 near Bridport, in the chimney of a local clergyman's cottage.)

An Egyptian skull with holes made for the removal of the brain before embalming.

Number 120 is the mummy of an infant, 121 the mummy of a cat.

A piece of skin found nailed to an ancient church door in Hedstock, Essex, in East Anglia, and taken from a Danish raider who had been flayed.

Strap-and-buckle tourniquets used in the Crimean War, and Savigny's field tourniquet. (With it the French surgeon LeCat could guillotine a leg at midthigh in forty-five seconds.)

I am nothing if not compulsively devoted to detail (indispensable to a museum guide), and thus am setting down the entries of this journal of Nicholas Szilich just as they were written, and with no attempt to editorialize. *Res ipsa loquitur.*

December 8, 1926

Twenty years ago I, Nicholas Szilich, was enrolled at the University Medical College in London. Like the poet Keats, however, one day I arose from my chair and gazed out the skylight of the great stone laboratory, to see a sunbeam roving there. Soon it had struck and held me in its shine, and therein I could see a host of elves and spirits floating, beckoning. I rose, as I say, and climbed up that sunbeam, never to return. In short, I became a poet.

For ten years the Muse garlanded my brow as easily as does this mistletoe the forest oaks. During this Golden Age I was to produce not only my two unpublished novels, "The Tongue of the Antelope" and "The Eye Unlidded," but my single book of poems, "Manna," as well. Like Keats again, I had fears only that I might cease to be before my pen had gleaned my teeming brain.

Then one day, with the suddenness of a natural disaster, my image-maker was gone. For ten years I have awaited the return of inspiration. These ten years have seen me employed as a guide in the Museum of the Royal College of Surgeons, a position that I was forced to take in order to keep food in my mouth. As for my writing, I am full of beginnings, bad ones. Here is one such:

The daybroken forest shivered, gasped, remembering the endless passionate night when great heated cats crouched in its branched groins, pressing their irritable hindparts against the bark to cool them, so to wait for the search for the other, and at last glassy fissures met above the whimper of need. There was the mount all biting, rending, plunging, release. Remembering this and all the others that rose in the dark like music, the forest slowly stretched, sweating dew, twisting the last drops of delight into memory, and to him that watched at dawn it seemed to shiver and gasp.

And this:

The marriage had become like a sick plant, the floor about which is strewn with fallen stalks. The last showy bloom was a dried brown cluster of cells, like an abandoned hornet's nest, cold and crackling to the touch. Its illness had been long and chronic; oh, not without small remissions when, muting his despair, he had fed and watered it with his semen, his blood. Then he would watch, mad with hope, as the night blooms appeared. They rarely lasted until morning, blinking out with the stars, as far away and as irretrievable. Now, of course, he was too tired for such embraces. And in any case his sex had turned as cold as his heart.
   "I do not love you," he said.
   "I never loved you," she said.

January 15, 1927

   I have lived too long in the absence of miracles. There is no point to it. In the old days, when the picture in my mind went dark and I was left as I am now, staring inward, searching for the faintest ray which might herald the emblazoning of imagination—when it did not come then, I had, in the old days, recourse. There was drink and women, and the clear fresh knowledge that there were decades ahead in which the spring would surely burble up on the ground again. So much time ahead! And indeed it *had* returned and each time it had been like a glory, all gold and luminescence and shimmer. But it has been ten years now since I have lived apart from my vision. In a wild state, yearning. At the end of each day I am as I was at the beginning. There is no way in, no trail, no spoor of unicorn to follow.
   I would go to any length, take any risks, for example incur any disease. I have for a long time held close to me the intuition that certain diseases produce an inflammation of the brain which, although insufficient to erupt into full clinical flamboyance, is still of such a chronic smoldering nature as to maintain a constant state of fever in the tissues. It is this irritation that I believe

6

to be beneficial to the creative impulse, stirring, abrading, kneading the cells to enzymatic excesses otherwise unknown. Translated into words these are the poems of the tuberculous Keats, the tales of the phthisic Chekhov, of the syphilitic Verlaine, the epileptic Dostoevsky. I considered becoming infected, but in the end I gave it up. I simply could not. Too fastidious.

June 6, 1927

Today I declared myself a Druid. It is the only way, there being no other of this persuasion to give me instruction or test, to receive or deny me. It is not, as you might think, a frivolous decision, but the consummation of months of religious study in which mysticism and ritual were my special interests. The choice was not easy. First eliminated were all religions extant and still practiced, for example Christianity, Judaism, and Islam. They are for the most part inanimate, overly spiritualized and abstract. Too, they are quite used up as far as miracles go. All is reduced to mere coincidence and chance. Excused also were all religions whose nature and symbols were so foreign to my European heritage that I would not internalize the flavor, "feel" the holiness. That took care of all Oriental, African, or other tribal practices. What I needed was something Indo-European, whose origins were shrouded in mystery and about which almost nothing of fact remains. After all, I am not and have never had pretensions to be a scholar, and nothing bores me more than digging out facts in a library. I wanted latitude, to take the framework, if you will, of an ancient cult, and plant a vine of my own choosing to wind in it. What was needed was something foresty, with stone altars, sacrifices, incantations, priests. Something druidic, I thought, and knew in an instant and beyond any doubt that I must be a Druid. It was so right for me.

There are still forests in Europe and in the offshore islands—no, I shall not tell you where—into which man has not pushed, which still retain the necessary solitude, the loftiness. There is one nearby, an easy walk from this town. Only the most energetic hiker would insist upon reaching the deepest portions, which are indeed severe with underbrush and in perpetual gloom. Yet I traversed it length and breadth, then length and breadth again, until I found the perfect place, the very heart of the thicket, near a narrow stream where a small natural clearing had formed from the fall of three or four trees. Scattered around the perimeter of the clearing were species of mushrooms, balled at the base and flowering into wicked penile heads. Several boulders, two large and one flat, formed the centerpiece of this circle. I set about clearing an area of ground, chopping and hauling the brush into the adjacent forest. When the diameter reached thirty feet I was finished. There was a perfectly concealed forest temple, the trees themselves pillars, rising in graceful archery to a living dome. The three boulders needed not to be touched, and are in fact uncannily good for the altar, the flat one being set between the two mounding ones.

I preferred to enter the clearing by crossing the narrow stream which coursed along one edge of it. For this purpose I had brought two flat boards which, laid side by side, reached across as a little bridge. Each time I crossed there was the liquid music made by my feet on these loose boards over the stream. It evoked a Proustian idea of standing on a slanted deck in some far-off water. And each time I stepped to the inner bank, it was like emerging from an estuary to face a vast gleaming sea.

With that, I set to the elaboration of a ritual. There were to be morning and evening chants, with specific incantations for each, although not too rich a litany. Repetition, you see, is valued for its hypnotic effect. On the first of each week and on feast days (of which there were none as yet, the first to be the anniversary of the enactment of the miracle), there was to be a sacrifice—live or a fresh kill. This would be presented to The God in the form of smoke. The symbol of The God is to be, naturally enough, mistletoe, a thing which thrives on ether alone and which, although not abundant, is found in these parts.

To how many men is it given to build a temple? It was with a feeling of elation that I began the task of clearing the ground. This elation was soon joined by a reverence as the faith itself began to settle in, as though with each passing hour of my work The God filled this natural chamber with a denser and denser cloud of His presence.* Yes, I disinter an ancient faith, resurrect a mossy old God moldering and rimy, build him an altar in the forest and write incantations to him, chant, solemnize, sacrifice, and perhaps—just perhaps—a thankful God would grant a miracle to His founder? God is anything but an ingrate, and founders do have certain rights. At least, they seem to have done rather well.

August 28, 1927

I am absolutely convinced that the coming of Lars was the onset of the miracle. I had left the forest at dusk after performing the evening ritual before the sacred stones. The sacrifice had burnt to a pile of ashes, and the smell of the rabbit flesh was awakening an irreverent hunger in me. I chanted the syllables, appealing for a successful night sea crossing, that the sun might journey beneath the sea all the night through, to emerge across the firmament at its rising place.

On my way home I stopped at a tavern for a glass of ale and to feel the warmth of men's presence in the room. There were perhaps a dozen there, miners and lorry drivers. There was no boisterousness, only a tired gray slouching against the bar, and silent drinking. It was too early in the evening. Later, veins

*Diodorus Siculus (*Hist.* V, 31, 225), ref. Druids of ancient Gaul.

dilated with beer would pump songs and laughter out of newly comic mouths. But now it was still, weighty in the alehouse. I saw him sitting alone at a table at one end of the room. Even in his heavy work jacket and peaked cap there was a difference about him I could sense. He looked part only of the silence—as for the rest, he was alone, separate, his blond hair gleaming beneath the cap, his eyes blue with intellect, his mouth a cynical bow. How my heart leaped! At the instant our eyes met, I felt a wave of faintness, a vertigo, through which came the sound of incantatory phrases echoing in a forest clearing. I knew it was a sign. I approached the young man.

"Good evening," I said. "May I join you?"

Only his eyes moved and for a long moment I was not sure, wondered if my fervor had not steered me wrong. Then he smiled, rupturing the hard curve of that upper lip like crystal into radiance.

"Please do. I would like some company."

"Szilich," I said. "Nicholas Szilich."

"Lars Nilsson."

We shook hands, mine scurrying into his large bright one like a small animal.

That night, our talk ranged from the Spanish writers—Pío Baroja and Unamuno—to the Lake Poets and Norse mythology. About each he was knowledgeable and sensitive. I could scarcely contain my excitement. As we parted for the night, I extended an invitation to dine at my house on the following evening.

August 29, 1927

All day I have prepared, with the care of a master chef, a list of subjects dear to my heart; committed to memory a series of interjections designed to lead him deeper and deeper into discussion. I mean to learn his brain. In the morning at dawn I went into the forest, to the altar, and recited the full litany for half an hour, at the end of which I placed a wooden cage of three larks on the stone altar and surrounded it with a pile of twigs. The flames agitated the stones with light and shadow.

September 3, 1927

I do not yet know the shape of the miracle, but have no doubt that it shall be revealed to me in time.

September 11, 1927

Ah, there is no time of life more salubrious than that spent waiting for a miracle. A hush, an expectancy lies over all the comings and goings of the day. I am one who, by nature, is not content to sit by and wait inertly for Fate or the Gods or Fortune, what have you, to turn benevolently toward me. I am a seizer, a reacher-out. I have always felt it important to place oneself in a position of advantage, so that should there be a happy direction, at the least I shall not have obstructed the path. Thus I leave my forest temple each evening in a state of contentment that to all the sitters and yearners of the world might seem pathologically inappropriate. For the past year I have set the stage for the miracle with a painstaking singleness of purpose. For example, tonight, according to the prescribed litany, I recited the incantatory phrases, the sacred Tla, followed by the ul at C above middle C and narrowing out to a fine hemiquaver. The echo of my voice returning to me from the forest canopy was nothing short of thrilling. I love incantations. They are my favorite words. After all, what other form infers —no, demands—the intervention of a supernatural being? I love the chant. For me it is no chore but a sublime privilege which often as not transports me out of myself.

September 15, 1927

This journal I mean to be the last statement of Nicholas Szilich as myself. I leave it because I cannot bring myself to do as other prophets and saints have done who have leaped the chasm between reality and myth. I feel duty bound to hand down to mankind, even as my body soars into the new magic —to hand down, as I say, the steps, mundane, pragmatic as they are, by which I, Nicholas Szilich, have dreamed, willed, and in fact brought about this overleaping.

I know now what I am to do. I dare not materialize it into words.

October 1, 1927

Today I have removed the brain from a sheep. It was surprisingly bloody and my awkwardness alarms me. I attribute this to a lack of experience. The whole procedure took six hours, far too long. I shall do one each week until I am ready.

October 9, 1927

The second sheep was sacrificed. It goes well. Operating time: four hours fifteen minutes.

In my first sheep experiment I held the head tightly between my knees, but have since found that a pair of tongs similar to those used to carry cakes of ice is perfectly suited to stabilize the head during the dissection. These are embedded in either temple. By grasping the handle one can turn the head to either side or lift it as necessary. This is my own refinement in technique and, perhaps immodestly, I refer to it as the Szilich maneuver. Necessity truly is the mother of invention. How happily I have confirmed that lovable old maxim!

October 19, 1927

I am ready. The third sheep took two hours and fifteen minutes. I cannot but feel it is The God who is guiding my hands. I have written a work sheet to follow if necessary, although each step is fixed in my memory. It follows herewith in this journal.

Removal of a Brain

To remove a brain takes two hours and fifteen minutes. It is like any other craft that can be routinized. There are steps which, if carried out methodically and with precision, lead to a successful conclusion. Of course it is understood that the tools or instruments must be of the highest caliber and in perfect condition. An entire day is set aside for sharpening and oiling the saw and burr.

1. The incision. This is a curvilinear cut, extending around the back of the scalp just behind the occiput, from temple to temple. It is deepened to the bone, making certain that the knife blade is held perpendicular to the tissues.

2. Raising the flaps. The first consists of the entire scalp anterior to the incision, and it is raised from the cranium and peeled forward as far as the eyebrows, where it remains attached. The posterior flap is carried back to the nape. A broad chisel is the best instrument for this.

3. The burr holes. These are four in number, two on each side of the head, placed far enough to the front and back so that the greatest expanse of cranium is included within a rectangular line drawn to connect these. These holes are the size of a sixpence and are made with a drill to which a rounded burr has been attached.

4. Lifting of the calvarium (so aptly named for the skulls

found strewn among the stones of Calvary). Once the windows have been completed, the brain is visible for the first time. A Gigli saw, which is little more than a flexible twisted wire with teeth embedded in it, is passed from one hole to another, taking great care not to scrape the brain. When both ends of the wire saw are protruding from adjacent holes, handles are attached to the looped ends, and the saw is drawn back and forth repeatedly until the bone has been transected. It is best during this maneuver to pour water on the skull occasionally to lubricate the saw. This must be done four times, of course, until all four apertures are connected. Any hooked tool may be used to elevate the island of bone now settled onto the underlying brain. This is done on both sides simultaneously, so as not to impale the brain with either edge. Now the entire top of the brain is visible.

5. The disengagement. This must be done with infinite gentleness. The fingers of the left hand are inserted between the front of the brain and the skull and slid in until the attachments of the dura mater offer resistance. With the organ thus palmed, the tough membrane is cut with scissors. This is done circumferentially.* One by one the nerve trunks which course from the undersurface through the foramina of the skull are similarly divided. Last to be severed is the spinal cord, just below the medulla oblongata. The brain is now free.

6. Removal. In a standing position and with the operator bending over the head, both hands are inserted into the skull on either side. It is important to slide the fingers well below the base of the brain, so that it can be lifted symmetrically and effortlessly, without the slightest force. The skull is now empty and the brain is cradled in the hands. It is carried to a basket of dried holly leaves and mistletoe, into which it is settled.

7. Reconstruction. The vault of the cranium is filled with wood chips and sawdust and tamped. The bone island is re-

*De corpore humani, Vesalius.

14

placed and the scalp flap repositioned. The incision is then sewn with a needle and heavy thread. Finally the hair is washed, dried, and combed neatly.

October 22, 1927

A portent! Today at exactly 7:37 A.M. I passed two stools, each in the shape of a perfect little sea horse. Enchanting! They swung dreamily upright in the bowl, nodding their heads. I have trained myself to be alive to these visitations. A state of heightened receptivity is of the utmost importance. Tomorrow! I suggested a walk in the forest to L. He was delighted. We meet here at dawn. I have decided to take him into my confidence, to make of him not only victim but conspirator, perpetrator as well. This I shall do when we reach the clearing. It would be injudicious before. In the pocket of my leather jacket is the wire cord, looped and twisted into handles at either end.

October 23, 1927

"What do you think, Lars?" I stole a glance at his face, terrified of his reaction yet strangely confident. He was hatless and wearing a short leather jacket, unbuttoned in front, although the autumn chill was penetrating. He was reclining on one elbow and one hip, the upper hip flexed for balance. I have never seen an elk, much less an elk lying down, but it must be such as this: a blend of grace and strength. Couchant, regardant, as they say. His expression changed slowly, as though his face were clearing itself of a mist. I saw that the curve of his mouth had tightened into a line, and when at last he looked up at me, it was to say, "I'm going away tonight. Good-bye. I do not believe, still . . ." Here his voice became pensive, dreamy.

I had moved to stand just behind him where he lay. My heart was pounding. I was sweating heavily yet felt penetrated by cold. An agitation was rising in me, starting in my legs and advancing upward. As it passed, my muscles—even my fat and skin—contracted into chaotic spasms. It was as though a great abrasive tongue were licking the inside of my body, leaving a terrible hunger there. When it reached the fingers of my right hand it was painful. The wire! I removed it from the pocket of my coat. The end loops fell eagerly, smoothly over my fists. I sank to one knee behind Lars and raised my manacled hands to the sky and with priestly deliberateness brought them down, the wire tight around his neck. There was no struggle, no rage, no foam, no wild bulge. Just a tension drawing out into a limpness. I held him for a long time, then lowered his head to the forest floor. When I turned him onto his back, leaves were stuck to the moisture of his lips. There was much to do.

I shall not detail the steps of the operation but refer the reader to the previously outlined technique. I shall, however, make brief but pointed commentary on each event.

1. The incision. The blood was disquietingly warm, and so much! It was necessary to concentrate again on the dry holly leaves—so settling to the stomach—and chant the first seven verses of the Braliddiul in order to calm myself.

2. Raising the flaps. This part went extremely well. There was a moment at the end, when the anterior flap was pulled down over the face, that was quite comical. In this position a hank of hair crosses the face at nose level as an exaggerated mustache. I laughed aloud at this point!

3. The burr holes. The odor of freshly ground bone is distinctive. For some time I have been trying to compare it with something else. It came to me suddenly. It is the odor of semen, yes, very much like it and thus like nothing else. I find this idea nostalgic.

4. Lifting of the calvarium. For the first time I saw the brain. O holy! holy! holy!

5. The disengagement. I scarcely breathed during this, and found myself literally gasping for air at its conclusion. With the

16

brain stem cut, the fruit falls free.

6. Removal. It is in my hands, cradled! A small perfect cloud, a pure crouching rabbit, the heart of a saint.

7. Reconstruction. Neatness and dignity are all.

Toward the brain I bent, taking its substance upon my lips and into my mouth. It had the consistency of a thick custard, and was salty. Close in I could smell the freshness of the kill. The remainder, in its basket, I placed in the flames.

To quaff wine from the skull of one's foe, or, as certain savages do, devour the slain enemy's heart, gives one complete ascendancy over him. It is not entirely a new idea, but I take the full credit for the brilliance of its execution. It is not mere low animal acquisitiveness, but an act of pure spirituality, for he who feeds upon the organs, or uses them for his own purposes, takes on the valor, the skill, and in this case the genius of the victim.

October 23, 1927 (later)

I awoke in the forest before the altar. Nearby on the ground lay this journal, whose last entry is the one you now read. The recent fire had burned to a small mound of ashes from which the last wisps of smoke wound, as though inhaled from above. (The God?) I recalled at once the circumstances of my coming to this place, the conversation with Szilich, his agitation (have I not felt the same at the moment of release?). There was the movement behind me. I think that I raised my neck, even held it out. To make it easier. He was so nervous. The bite of the wire was hard but I have felt worse pain. It's all in the giving in, the resignment. Rolling with it. And now it has worked! They will not find me out. I can stop running. Hidden forever in the body of another man. Never to be found. I buried Szilich in the depths of the forest. Of my own crime I do not wish to speak.

17

The Consultation

He walked the center aisle of the convention hall, past stands of textbooks on *Surgical Anatomy, Complications of Surgery, Peripheral Vascular Diseases—Their Diagnosis and Treatment.* Other stalls gleamed with instruments—rows of proctoscopes, bronchoscopes, gastroscopes, rigid with potential, awaiting on one end a palpitating orifice, on the other a knowing eye. Here were forceps, clamps of the finest dentition. He tried one in his hand, listening to the impeccable click as the ratchets locked tight, tighter, tightest, a sound that had both frightened and comforted him all his professional life. There were scalpels of superior edge, their silver bellies as diverse as tropical fish, and retractors for holding open incisions, retractors of such cleverness as to match the ingenuity of a royal armorer.

Suddenly he was bored with it, the lectures, the instruments, the whole gadgetry of surgery, the rooms full of well-dressed men who all looked forty-five years old. . . . He would call her up.

She had a shockingly virtuous telephone voice which placed the brief arrangements over price in the grossest ill taste.

"Shall I pick you up at your hotel?"

"Fine."

"Oh, yes. Dinner first?"

"I'd love to. Where?"

"You choose it."

"What time?"

"Seven-thirty be all right?"

"Fine. Looking forward. . . ."

The illusion of romance was under way.

Gloria Snurkowski was the name he had been given to look up. He had laughed then at the idea of a Polish prostitute. Still, she had to be *something*. He was reassured when he saw her an hour later in the lobby of the hotel, serpentine, icy, impeccably dehumanized. Except for one thing—a gesture. Now and then she would place the third and fourth fingers of her hand to the corner of her mouth and press them against the underlying teeth. It was a Polish peasant's move. He was certain that her grandmother had done it a thousand times in the middle of her wheat field. But that was the only thing she had overlooked. The rest was perfect.

In the morning he had awakened first. One eye was buried in the pillow but with the other he followed the tide of her breathing. She was lying on her side, part of her back resting against him. A golden stripe of sunshine appeared abruptly between two slats of the Venetian blind and lit up the mountain range of her shoulder. His eye skied down her neck, leaped off the ridge of her clavicle, and descended to the upper slope of the breast in a squinting shower of light. His vision paused for a moment at the foot of the slope, then moved on up the smooth ascent, slowly, gradually, passing through a small shaded declivity, then up again into the sunlight toward the nipple. He held it there until the strain of looking so far to the side made itself felt, then relaxed, and sped down the far side. Halfway down, his vision was jarred by a small rise. Automatically, he backed up the hill like a rewinding movie, then flicked the switch and let it go again. There, where the bump was on the trail, the skin was different, pitted by a shallow dimple. He

19

raised his left arm to bring his hand around to the breast, and palmed it carefully. When she did not stir, he moved his fingers to the southern slope, sounding the depths as he went. He was moving over the rough spot now, his fingers growing exploratory, aggressive, deft. He picked up tissue between thumb and fingers, rotating it, fathoming. She moaned in discomfort, still asleep.

A cold white knowledge drifted into his mind like a snowfall, each flake of which was a bit of evidence. The lump was hard. It was discrete. It was irregular in shape. It was fixed to the overlying skin, fixed as well to the underlying muscle. It was immovable. It was tender. And his palpating fingers fled from her body like frightened fish in a pond. The suddenness of their departure was what fully awakened her.

He swung his feet to the floor and padded across the carpet to the bathroom, where he showered long and deliberately. He dried himself and went back to the bed, where he sat down and reached for his socks on the floor. She turned, and one of her hands reached around his waist, dipping.

"You're getting dressed?"

"Yes, I've got to be going."

With his back to her, he said, "I've got to talk to you."

"It's a hundred dollars."

"No, no, I don't mean that. I mean, that's O.K., a hundred dollars. Here." He reached for his wallet, counted out a fifty and five tens, and held it out to her.

She raised up on one elbow, watched this very carefully, and said, "Put it on the table." Then she sank back and watched him dress.

"You're buttoning your shirt wrong. You missed one."

He unbuttoned it and started again from the bottom. "There's something I've got to tell you," he began again.

"You're not sick, are you?" She was paying attention now.

"No, I'm not." . . . A pause. "But you are."

"What do you mean?"

"Listen. I'm a doctor, as you know." His voice took on a deeper, more professional tone, but his armpits were wet. "I couldn't help but feel . . ." Her open naïve mouth, her eyes wide and waiting . . . "You've got a lump in your breast." He couldn't turn away from her.

Her face stayed vacant.

"A lump. I felt it. Right side."

She moved from her elbow to her back, settling onto the bed.

"Here." He picked up her hand as though it were a cup of coffee, and guided it to her breast. Holding the fingers, he led them toward the spot and pressed them down, moving them in a circular fashion. Her face changed slowly, tightened around enlarging eyes. Her lips were closed and dry.

"Do you feel it?"

She nodded slightly. "Yes."

"You've got to see a doctor. It must be taken care of."

"What is it?"

"I don't know." He shrugged and turned away. "Maybe it's nothing."

"It's something, isn't it?"

"I don't know. You can't tell until it's removed."

"You know."

"I don't know, I tell you."

"You're a doctor. You know. If it is, what do they do?"

He hadn't meant to go this far. "If it isn't, there's only a small scar. It won't show."

"And if it is? They will take off my breast." It was said as an announcement, flatly, without inflection. "I won't do it."

"You have to. It's important."

She covered her breasts with her arm, protectively, the palm of one hand gripping the opposite shoulder.

"Doctor." She was strange to him, formal, as though she had not just a few hours before felt him explode against her. "I can't do that."

"Look, I'm talking about your life, not your livelihood."

Their voices were low, surreptitious. They knew only words of one syllable. It was as though they kept them that way, afraid that if they raised them, spoke out loud, their sentences would crumble into meaningless noises.

"What is it? Tell me."

"I don't know."

"You ought to."

"But I don't."

"What should I . . . ?"

"It needs to come out."

"No!"

"Be sensible. It might be . . ."

"Cancer."

She had said it first. All along it had been a game, not unlike choosing sides by gripping a baseball bat to see who wins first choice. He had won; she had said it first. She reached for her slip and shyly lowered it over her head, then with small furtive movements she put her arms through the strap holes. There was about her the caved-in look of the victim. It made him vaguely nauseated. Not the strangeness of the word; certainly he knew it over and again in his daily work. Nor the translation of it into suffering. But rather what sickened him was the thought that he and the lump had been rivals, each feeding on her flesh, reaching within her, that they had been competing for her in a kind of race to have her before the other could use her all up, leaving none.

His fingers scuttled to the doorknob and locked around it like pincers. He turned to find her eyes fixed on his hand now palming the doorknob.

22

"Well, good-bye. Be sensible, now. You can only tell under the microscope. Anyway, it's a small price to pay in exchange for your life."

Her eyes never wavered from that doorknob, which was a hard lump in his hand. With sudden violence he twisted it as hard as he could and pulled as though to avulse it from the wood.

"Wait!" She walked to the table and picked up one of the ten-dollar bills. "Here. Thanks for the consultation." She was smiling just a little now.

He matched her smile, but his mouth was dry. "Sorry," he said softly then. "I don't make house calls."

Train Ride

It had been capricious of him to do it, and despite earlier moments of happy wickedness, he began to feel foolish and guilty. He had done nothing for so long, gone nowhere, that when the idea of a train ride occurred to him, he had seized it and was surprised at the strength of the impulse. He was surprised, too, that it had lasted more than a few minutes.

Ordinarily, fatigue, the brutal fatigue that encased him brain and limb like a humid cloud, made short work of his plans. He had occasionally a surge of enthusiasm for something, a book, the piano, an hour of gardening, but no sooner had he begun to think about the project than would come the ebbing of all energy, and he was left moist and impotent on a deck chair in the garden. It was all he could do to sit still and keep from giving in to his despair.

He was in that deck chair when the thought of the train ride first occurred to him. His eyes closed, he was listening to the garden, especially the sound of the trees brandishing their branches, straining to roar, but achieving only a listless sighing. He was certain that they were mad with restlessness, hating the roots that knotted them in place, the stiff unbending trunk.

The far-off sound of a train whistle came to him as though he had been expecting it. He shuddered and struggled to remember something he had heard once, or read, about the sound of a horn in the depths of the forest. The sound was a promise and he waited then for something to happen. But there was only the noise of the leaves.

Gardening was his hobby; more, his second life. He needed to garden and he did it by habit in all his spare time, when strength allowed. The earth drew him down on his knees again and again to swallow his hands. But he had a peasant's resentment of the earth, too. He hated it for having forced him to his knees, into spending his strength in it. He had thought then, I live always just a little bit above the ground, even digging into it as if to get in all the way. But he gardened when he could.

I'll take a train ride, he thought. Somewhere, not too far, no specific destination, just a train ride. The idea was breath-taking, audacious. To move swiftly across the country again, whipping past the landscape. He was exhilarated. Slowly, resolutely, he swung his legs to the ground and sat up. Everything he did was slow and resolute. He hooked a finger into his vest pocket, caught a small tin box, and placed a tablet under his tongue. Then, pushing off with his arms, he stood up and brushed the maple seedlings from his trousers.

At the railroad station he bought a round-trip ticket and a newspaper, before moving to the platform to wait. He took another pill as the train smashed by him, coming to a halt in a little miracle of friction. Once aboard, he took an aisle seat, thinking, I must sit somewhere near the toilet. He had thought often in recent months of the sly migration of one's preoccupation from the bedroom to the kitchen to the bathroom, and even named the progress the "house tour of decay." Congratulating himself as the train pulled away, he looked about at the passengers near him. They displayed a bored gracefulness that he found quite beautiful. They were all so skillfully alive.

Today, he thought, I am a passenger, too.

The train was grinding through the country, and he sat back and listened with envy to its regular pulse. Presently, sleep rose from his legs.

"Is there a doctor in this car?"

It was a woman's voice, stern, staccato. He turned to see her striding down the aisle, her black hair drawn into a tight ball at the back, under a conductor's cap. The *plock* of her heels preceded her, and he was not surprised to observe that they were extraordinarily high, sharp, and patent leather. Her skin was white as an oyster shell, unrelieved by the slightest color, although her lipstick was so dark as to seem black against her pallor. Her eyes jerked from side to side, scanning the rows of seats. Every few seconds the plocking skipped a beat as she lurched against a seat and then fell back into stride. She was a few rows behind him now and he watched with the same detachment. As the breeze from her passage brushed his cheek, he spoke.

"I'm a doctor."

He was not even sure it was his voice that he heard. He could not remember having used his mouth to speak. She turned.

"You're a doctor?" It was a demand as much as a question.

"Yes."

"Follow me, please. There is someone who needs you in the rear car."

He rose to his feet as though pulled by a string. To his surprise, the fatigue had lifted and he was moving expectantly along the aisle after her. Imagine it, he thought. To be useful again! He was rushing to practice his skill! He felt the eyes of others upon him. After all, he had identified himself to the crowd.

A vision of himself rose in his mind as they progressed down the aisle, she stabbing imperiously at the floor, he moving resolutely out of habit. He fixed his eyes on the back of her head, aware that the faces of the passengers were turning like riffled pages as he passed.

He remembered riding the ambulance as an intern, crouching by the stretcher in the back, the siren an emblem in his head. He saw again the cars pulling to the side to let him through. They were like cattle, turning in unison to nose away from the dog that herds them. They were the faces that turned to him now as he moved down the aisle behind her.

At the end of the car she pulled the door open. It required a great effort to overcome its suction, and she tugged at it, her legs braced apart. Already through the passageway, she had barely held the door open until his own hand took it from her in midclosure. He was panting now and sweat had begun to form on his face. It had become uncomfortably hot and he was straining to keep up the pace. They were lurching down the aisle of the second car and he clutched at the seat backs, using his arms to push off. The white leaves riffled slowly and a second door was torn open. A wave of dizziness took him and he was pulled wildly from side to side, falling forward toward the woman. Her eyes, when she turned once to make certain that he was following, were black as garnets above the garnet gash of her mouth.

He was in a panic by the time they reached the third car. A pain had sprung in his elbow and was burrowing up the arm. Still she marched, and it seemed to him in the fourth car that he would die here. The thought appalled him. It was undignified to die in public, to crumble and fall before strangers, travelers, who would pass this spot in a month or a year and say, "He died here." To thud down in transit, unknown, inviting stares, a few whispers, and later a story at lunch—"Someone died on the train today"—was not possible.

They were in the sixth car. How many more were there? How many more could he make? A fist gripped his chest and tightened. Something essential beneath his breastbone was being squeezed. He fumbled for his vest pocket and the tin of pills. Where was it? Each time his fingers touched the box he would be thrown sideways into a seat, once falling across a man's lap. He was steadied by upraised arms and passed on to the next, like a baton from runner to runner.

There was a sound in his ears. It had begun so subtly as to be unnoticed, rising in pitch with his effort and exhaustion. It sounded like a single note played on a cello. At the beginning of the seventh car, he had the pillbox and was groping with the cover. It would take both hands to open it. He would have to let go of the seats, and this he would do quickly, in a single second, while his body hung like a dancer at the top of his leap. He would wait for the next thrust of the car. There! He let go and pried the tiny lid. It was done. He had it! He could see them arranged in the box.

With a sudden jerk of the train the box flashed from his hand, scattering the tiny pills like leaves gusted from a tree. Something settled in him and he was blown forward. Before him danced the hard shining ball of her hair. The door swung open, what car he could not remember. Its closing shoved him forward.

The conductor pointed downward, her rigid finger gleaming red at the tip.

"There."

No longer able to focus his vision, he saw only a dark, man-sized smudge on the floor. He fell headlong into it as the train came to a halt.

Fairview

My dearest Vera,

There is such a bustle and stir at the hotel. It is as though we will be visited today by an important personage. A queen or an archangel or, wild wild hope, by you, my darling. Nothing else would do to explain the "high" that one senses here today. A dozen times have I turned from my book (although it has spice enough to mesmerize de Sade) to peer expectantly down the road. Even the lilies at the gate are bobbing and ducking to get a better view. Perhaps we should all look up, as I should not be surprised if our guest were to arrive from on high—one of your silvery astronauts carrying a tiny planet for his son, or a rug merchant from Tabriz riding smugly on his merchandise. Won't he be put down to learn this hotel doesn't take used furnishings? The swank fairly oozes from the walls. I myself shall inform the cheeky carpet beggar that even the beds are discarded each morning. We never use anything twice! Well, we shall simply have to pocket our watches (pun) and try to keep from going mad with anticipation. Be still, my heart, and all that. Perhaps a walk will help. My neighbor here is an indefatigable walker. Not heath nor steppe, not veldt nor mesa is safe from his clodhoppers. All, all he violates with his lecherous prancing. No virgin territory here. Not on your life. Old Richardson has taken care of that with his mindless laying waste. I myself am an ambler, a meanderer. I just don't like to butt into Nature's business. She knew what she was about, arranging her grass and her sand that way. It doesn't need my boot to sock it askew. No, ma'am. I'll slither through the blades like a little green snake, leaving it all arranged just as she put it, or melt away a morning on a barnacle-bearded rock in the tide waiting for a mollusk to open wide and say "Aaah." But Richardson and I are good for each other. We even look well together, I'm sure. So, of course, we would have to wear each other like apparel for the benefit of the lobby. He is big and red with white sideburns, and I—well, you know what I look like.

Oh, Vera, hurry back to me. Man cannot live forever by whimsy and caprice. And I must get back to the serious work of my life—you, my magnum opus, my unicorn. There is so much left unfinished. The two spots I have neglected to kiss, the one on your neck beneath your earlobe—luckily I have forgotten which one, and will have to do both for the sake of completeness—and the other on your left instep. I cannot have you sailing the seas uncovered by kisses lest some beetling Beelzebub find these heels of Achilles, and slay Love for me.

Your last letter should have been written in light on hummingbirds' wings. It is love perfused with air. To be loved by you is all in all.

Dr. Allain gunned his car up the winding road toward the Fairview Convalescent Hospital. There was not a jot of eagerness in him. He had not visited this one before, but knew well enough what to expect. They were of two types—one, darkly old with wrinkled antimacassars limp upon the chifforobes and samplers on the walls; the other, geometrically "decorated" in plastic and aluminum upon which no self-respecting germ would light. In general he disliked less the old converted houses with samplers that said IN GOD WE TRUST, or JESUS LOVES, or even GOD BLESS THIS PLACE. If he were to stitch one, it would say HELP, HELP right out. This type of convalescent home made no pretense. Just pack them in around the Victorian pieces and dust it all once a week.

He steered his car up the winding steep street atop which he would find the place. It had to be on top in order to justify the inclusion of the word "view" in its name. This one was Fairview. Others were Soundview, Bayview, Oceanview, Mountainview —all precursors, he mused dryly, of that ultimate convalescent home, Skyview, where the insurance never runs out.

Beyond which turn in the road would it become visible? Squat, flat-topped, with ramps like tongues sticking out of every orifice. He knew he had reached the site when he began to see them, here and there on the lawn, propped into deck chairs or standing immobile over canes like withered cornstalks. They would wait there peering through their cataracts, drooped and dripping, until attendants came, white and grim, to coax them back to Fairview. He pulled into the parking lot, driving very slowly, half expecting to find a stray strewn across the path. They seemed to have been flung about by an explosion. Getting them out of bed in the morning must be tantamount to disinterment, he thought. There it is, Fairview.

In front was a huge elm tree in the advanced stages of disease. It seemed devoid of life save for three or four courageous branches near the top, whose few leaves waggled still above the skeleton. The desiccated trunk teemed with fungi which burst through the bark like a horde of marauding goblins. It was in a state of virtual death, or technical life, depending on one's point of view.

He consulted the list of patients to be seen. Alvin Richardson was the first name: ulcer of foot.

"Where can I find Mr. Richardson?" he asked of the nurse at the desk.

"Room fifteen, doctor. I'll send someone down to assist you."

"Thank you."

He passed a long table in the lobby where a clutch of crones sat weaving colored ribbons into potholders. Others painted flowers on clay vases. The grave-smell of wet clay seemed appropriate. Perhaps they were here just to get used to it, he thought. He passed open doors on either side of the corridor, through which could be seen the still mounds of the bedridden. He heard stertorous breathing, noted the smell of feces and urine. There was a rich productive cough and the emphatic spit that followed like an exclamation point. He encouraged his step toward number fifteen. On the bed, all four extremities twisted and frozen into the shape of a pretzel, Alvin Richardson took no note of the doctor's arrival. He lay on his back staring at the tangle of his feet that hung suspended above his head like antlers. One was covered by a bandage moist with drainage from a concealed wound.

"Mr. Richardson?" He asked a tentative question. No response. He opened a package of instruments, the rubber gloves, and gauze squares, setting everything on the bedside table. He had developed an indecent curiosity about the contents of these night tables, upon which the patients piled all of their keepsakes, mementos, get-well cards, and edibles. This one was bare save for a lonely glass of faintly turbid water, one sip of which he was certain would lay him mad and frothing.

A nurse arrived and, leaning over the bed, grasped the leg to steady it while he unwrapped the soggy gauze. The odor of rot was strong and, the wound undressed, he could see the reason. A serpiginous ulcer wound along the entire side of the foot and across the sole. He donned the gloves and proceeded to attack the scab with scissors and forceps, cutting and pulling away the hidelike tissue.

"How long has this been present?" he asked the nurse, trying to keep reproach out of his tone.

"It's gone very fast, doctor. It wasn't there two weeks ago. He must have gotten himself into a bad position with his foot pressed against the railing somehow. Poor soul, but he moves

now and then, you know. We find him in the weirdest tie-ups."
She laughed ingratiatingly.

Bad boy, Mr. Richardson. You shouldn't move at all, he
thought. You should just lie still where you're put. Now see
where your rocking and wriggling have got you. A sore foot, and
with bone showing at the bottom. We'll be a long time getting
that in shape.

"Doctor, may I call the other girls? I want them to see this,
too."

"Of course."

Alone with the patient, he bent over the dead foot, directly
beyond which he could see the man's face. The eyes roved in
their fissures, briefly reconnoitering the operation above, then,
preoccupied with a fog of their own, moved on.

The first *pop* he did not hear, nor the second or third. It was
only later that he realized them back from below the threshold
of hearing. At the fourth or fifth *pop*, he began to wonder idly
what was causing it. The sounds were spaced irregularly, about
two to three minutes apart, and were not all of the same intensity, some being stronger than others. At the sixth *pop* he
turned and with a jolt realized that there was another person
in the room, a second or third, depending on how much one
emphasized Mr. Richardson.

He straightened completely, still holding the scissors and forceps in his gloved hands, and faced the intruder, or had he been
there all the time?

"I beg your pardon. I didn't see you. You startled me."

The man was sitting in a low wheelchair with his back to him.
He did not answer.

"I mean, have you been here all the time?"

In front of the wheelchair was an ancient typewriter, and as
he watched, an arm flung itself from the man's body, bending
and winding as though it had more joints than it should. Arched
at the wrist, rotating, flailing, it swung behind his head. Then

33

the other arm appeared, flying up to meet its fellow, steering by the same incomprehensible stars. As they struggled in the air, the huge head tipped forward on his neck, lolling between the shoulders, and turned to face the right hand, squinting to get it in his sights. With a sudden violent jerk the hand was brought down on the typewriter and, *pop,* the index finger struck a key. His body slumped and the arms settled slowly, sinuously to his sides.

Allain caught his breath. The man was typing! He was short. This Allain could discern despite the man's sitting position. His feet, encased in the heaviest of black shoes which came to the ankles, hung freely. The shoes were far from new, but strikingly unscuffed. Worn by no walker, they were either weights or ornaments. The voluminous trousers were black and suspended from his shoulders. He wore a gray undershirt from the orifices of which emerged two arms and a neck of whiteness so stark as to belie the presence of blood coursing beneath the surface. He had not yet seen the man's face. The right arm was again stirring, scurrying away from the torso, swinging up and out in a grandiose overshooting of the mark, falling in back of the bowed head. Again its fellow took sudden awkward flight and shot up to meet it. They tangled and turned in the air like birds. One, having spotted its prey, dipped, shuddered, then shot, finger extended, toward the key. *Pop* went the typewriter. The great head rose to eye the page and saw the doctor. His surprisingly red lips were pulled into a grimace that might have been a smile. To Dr. Allain they had the quality of bruised fruit.

"Hello." The doctor cleared his throat.

"Aow." The voice had the same lack of control as the arms. It gave the distinct impression that unless great care were taken, it would shoot off into outer reaches of sound that would terrify both listener and speaker.

"You're typing," he said blankly, aware at once of his awkwardness. "I am Dr. Allain. I've come to treat your roommate's bad leg."

After a long pause, during which he seemed to be gathering himself together, the man began to laugh. It took a few moments for Allain to define the unrestrained scraping in the throat and the heave of the shoulders as laughter. Why was he laughing? Allain wondered. Can it be that he sees some irony here—Richardson's foot, the nurse, my being here at all? Or was he merely embarrassed at being seen?

"What's your name?"

"A-Arold."

"Harold?"

"Ayss."

Allain wished ardently that he had not started the conversation. The man had not turned back to his typewriter, and seemed to be expecting more or, at least, waiting to see if any more would be said. So he was without embarrassment. It was Allain who was ill at ease.

Pardon me for intruding, he wanted to begin. I could not help but be impressed by your ability to type. But something like intelligence sparkled in the man's eyes, and he could not say it.

"Have you been here long?"

"Ayss."

"Where are you from?"

Again there was a pause, followed by the same shaking of shoulders and scraping laugh.

"Well, I've got to finish this job. Nice talking to you, Harold."

Harold did not shift his gaze, but continued to watch him, holding him.

"What are you writing?"

"A ledder."

"How long does it take you to type a letter?"

"A mon."

"A month?"

"Ayss."

From where he was standing, he could see that the page in the typewriter was three-quarters covered with type. He had moved to within a few feet of the man, and darted a glance at the page.

"My dearest Vera," he read.

My dearest Vera! God in Heaven! He's writing to a woman, calling her "my" and "dearest"! Allain's hands shook with a fine tremor. He inched closer, knowing that he would read the letter, knowing, too, that he would be seen; caring, but feeling a compulsion to do it. Within reading distance now, he quickly scanned the page. It was almost illegible, surrealistic. There were many letters crossed out with X's (costly). Words ran together without spacing, and whole lines slanted wildly.

When he finished, he looked down to see Harold, half turned, grinning up at him wetly through his purple lips. There was no accusation in that grin, no resentment. Only, again, an ambiguity. Allain stood silently, no longer embarrassed. It was as though the letter had broken down the experience into its component parts, stripped it of pretense and formality. They seemed to have discovered each other.

He looked at the night table near Harold's bed. It was a wasteland of tissues, postcards, loose crackers, and a carafe of water. In the center stood the framed photograph of a woman, glossy, dark. She was gazing coolly over the shoulder of the viewer, no trace of a smile on her perfect features. Her black-sequined gown dipped dangerously across her white bosom. In the lower right corner was written with a flourish:

"To Harold with love," and under that, "Joan Crawford."

Allain nodded slightly at the picture.

"Vera?" he asked quietly.

"Ayss." Harold grinned.

The Sympathetic Nose

Bartolomeo Vincenzi found it hard to live without his nose.

I know. I am Borgarucci, a servant in his household, and for one of my station, learned beyond all proportion. I can read and write with equal facility, and more graceful than my own pen in the copying of letters, there is none in Mantua. My father taught me this trade, and his father him. Before me, they were amanuenses. So you can see, I know all that goes on in this house —all business, prayer, and lechery—and of each there is no dearth, I assure you. But this which takes place here, and which I shall presently unfold to you, is surpassing strange, both tragickal and comical.

It was not merely the way his children turned aside when they spoke, and on some pretext or another absented themselves from the dining room. Often they ate in the kitchen with the servants. Even Emilia, my mistress, though she continued to sit at the opposite end of the great oaken table, seemed to have lost interest in her food. She would peer disconsolately in the steaming tureens and bowls set before her, only to wave them away with the deepest of sighing. His business associates, Messers Fioravento and Bandini, avoided his rooms for conferences. They sent emissaries and letters instead.

Even last Sunday, he was walking down the steps of the great Cathedral itself when he heard the children chanting from across the courtyard, loud enough for him to hear every word,

> Bartolomeo Vincenzi lost his nose,
> He does not look so well.
> And in its place he wears a rose,
> So still contrives to smell.

He had swept haughtily down the steps and across the piazza, pretending not to have heard, but his clenched fists and quivering beard surely must have given him away.

As was said, it was not just for these and many more instances of repudiation by family and townspeople that his life was now miserable. It was his feeling about himself. He felt so much less than he had been. One would think that the loss of such a small thing—a nose, after all—would not leave him so much diminished, but Bartolomeo felt the loss piercingly. It was as though *he* had been mowed off his nose, rather than the other way around, and his nose, although the lesser of the two fragments in bulk, had seceded from the whole with the lion's share of manhood. Perhaps his shame would not be so acute if he had not had so gorgeous a nose before. It had truly been an organ of prodigy, exciting marvel among men and lust among women. Each time he passed through the great front hall of his house he would gaze up at his portrait, a full-length representation by the great Grimaldi himself. He was shown in full ducal splendor with rich black robes over lace, and hung with heavy gold chains. But all the regalia failed to draw the viewer's eye from that splendid decoration which vaulted from its bridge in a flawless parabola, narrow above and fleshing out to a pair of sensuous fine-rimmed nostrils, each one a perfect pink and mysterious oval, through which were wafted to and fro the high and scented winds of aristocracy. He could not bear to look at the portrait. It was for him a mockery more cruel than that which could be devised by the foul and filthy populace out there. And had it not been because of them that he had lost his nose in the first place? He had contracted with the Master of Perugia to carve a statue of himself for the piazza.

"Not for any vanity, I assure you," agonized Bartolomeo. "Solely for the beautification of the city, so that one and all might look upon it with pride and admiration, that they might congratulate one another upon having the good luck to live in such a town, adorned by such a masterwork."

He had traveled to Perugia himself to select the marble to be used for the pedestal, and had been fortunate enough to buy a newly quarried rock of such a purity as to be reminiscent of the best Parian. White as cream it was, with here and there a swirl of palest rose.

It was on the return journey that it happened. Those brigands of Ravenna—devils, brutes—had been lying in wait, and as he and his party of fourteen servants and three coaches emerged from a brief glade, there was a sudden impact followed by shouts, and the neighing of the beasts. The carriage doors were torn open, and he was pulled by his sleeves and thrown to the ground.

"Slaves! Men!" he had shrieked. "Seize them! Fight! Defend me!" But the rascals lay on the earth where they had been knocked, and pretended to be dead. Not one rose to his aid. The pirates stripped the coaches of their contents, turned loose the horses, pulled off his rings and the great chain about his neck, the ruffians, and slashed his coat; even his boots felt the cut of their steel and hung in ridiculous shreds about his ankles. Aboil with rage, Bartolomeo ranted and cursed.

"You will pay for this! I am Bartolomeo Vincenzi! I shall hold Ravenna to account for this! Barbarians!"

At that, if a handsome young hoodlum had not strutted up, and grabbing Bartolomeo's nose between the thumb and fore-finger, his little finger raised delicately—if he had not with a great swiftness cut with his sword down upon the nose! I can still see the flash of the sun upon the blade as it swung and the young

Tartar's hand taking leave of Bartolomeo's face and taking with it Bartolomeo's nose.

In an instant the pirates were gone, and the servants—I among them—one by one rose, and waited for their master's declamation.

"Help me, fools! I die! I am lost!" he cried.

We ran to him, laid him upon the carriage, and with cloths and cool water from a stream placed compresses on his face, there where the nose had been. Some ran to retrieve the horses and, hitching the first two to the carriage, drove home at full tilt. The bleeding was furious. Bartolomeo was certain that he would exsanguinate before we reached his house.

The next morning, the wicked mirror that informed him of his noselessness lay smashed upon the marble tiles of his sitting room. For ten horrifying seconds Bartolomeo had faced his broken image and admitted that he was ugly, sphinxish. Then he had wept.

In a month the wound had healed. The edges rolled and contracted into a shamefully low triangular ridge where the nose had anchored to the face. Inside, the gaping orifice glowed red and moist and steamy. Each night Bartolomeo would beat his cheeks with his fists, and thrust himself about the room, crying:

"I shall not get up tomorrow, nor ever again."

But on February 14, 1584, as he sits at his writing table, gazing into the garden, he is up to something new. He is writing to Dr. Tagliacozzi.

Well you might ask who is Dr. Tagliacozzi, for his fame has not yet spread into the lesser cities of Italy. And only yesterday did Bartolomeo become aware of the existence of such a genius, an artist. Tagliacozzi is a surgeon of Bologna. He it is who was inspired to invent the operation of Restoration of the Nose. For have not noble noses been falling under the onslaught of the

French Disease? And now Bartolomeo is writing to Tagliacozzi. It is said that there are as many as twenty lords and soldiers living at his house in various stages of nasal reconstruction—so far have things gone in the general lapse of morality! Cupid's arrow strikes not the heart, but the nose. Hee-hee!

Thus, Bartolomeo wrote:

February 14, 1584

My illustrious, most excellent and honored Messer,

His Eminence Giulio, Cardinal Montaldo, my kinsman, has prompted me to enlist your consultation in the matter of my most uncomfortable indisposition. In a circumstance altogether heinous and barbarous, my person was attacked with weapons, and in the course of altercation I sustained the wound of Severance of the Nose, from which I still suffer despite the passage of twelve months. Word of your prowess in matters of bodily restitution having spread to the ears of His Eminence, in all sympathy he has urged me to present my case to you. May it please Your Honor to accord this wretched writer the healing touch of your hands which I kiss in closing.

Wishing you every true good.

BARTOLOMEO VINCENZI

from Mantua

And here is the reply:

March 2, 1584

My most illustrious and honored Messer,

It is pleasing to me to honor His Revered Eminence, your kinsman, in the matter of applying whatever knowledge I have toward the reconstruction of your nose. It would be of considerable convenience and pleasure to me should you arrive in Bologna, at my house, in the afternoon of the first day of Lent. May it please God to restore you to good health, and to grant you every other fulfillment of happiness, as I likewise desire for His Eminence Cardinal Montaldo. I kiss your hands.

GASPARE TAGLIACOZZI

from Bologna

41

My master writes further:

March 16, 1584
Most illustrious Messer Tagliacozzi,

His Eminence has gratefully appreciated the kind promptness with which Your Honor has offered his services in the correction of my most unhappy state. One aspect only of this proposed work gives me cause for hesitation and keeps me from long since having hurled myself upon your threshold, so hot is my ardor for your scalpel. I do confess to a certain distaste in the use of my own arm as the donor of the tissues. Lest this be construed as a lapse of courage or perseverance, may I suggest in all delicacy that, descended as I am through long lines of the nobility in which, in truth, there are not a few currents of royal blood, my own sensibilities have become so sharply honed, the nerves so refined that, receptive as is my flesh to the end of your benevolent knife (it trembles like a bride), I do suffer the pricks and pains of usage with an uncommon intensity. Therefore I do tell you that I am unable to bear what to coarser fabric would be a moderate discomfort, but which to my fine filigree would be a tearing beyond endurance.

Therefore, honored and esteemed sir, I earnestly beseech you to permit me the use of a slave for this purpose, to whom I have offered a handsome quantity of money, and manumission as well, in return for the flesh from his upper and inner arm. Such a one, Virax by name, have I in my employ, and indeed he is a grateful wretch for the opportunity to serve me in this way, and to gain his generous reward. I kiss your hands.

BARTOLOMEO VINCENZI

from Mantua

The next letter is written by my master from the hospital in Bologna:

April 15, 1584
Your Revered Eminence, my brother-in-law,

What an agony is this! Even as I write, the wretched slave finds new ways to torment me. Now he will flex his fingers, now clench and unclench his fist in order to send ripples of motion up his arm, which, arriving at that most sensitive of spots, the *locus minoris resistantiae*, lancinate my face in such a way as to cause me to utter shrieks and moans most piteous to hear. I ask you to envision only the most superficial portion of my Gehenna, never the full imagining of the true and depthless horror, lest your refined sensibility recoil too violently from it and you fall senseless in some unattended place. Yet bear with me a little of it since it comforts me to write.

It is three weeks since the Tagliacotius, himself a veritable architecture, nay, a labyrinth of complexities, stood before the dais on which I sat. The slave, this burly mound of brawn, was led in to stand behind my chair. (I tell you now, though I am shorn of nose, he is shorn of soul. Such a brute is there.) Many knaves and apprentice surgeons filled the surgery. One held a metal basin beneath my chin, in which to catch the blood. Another knelt upon my feet and, leaning over my knees, held fast my trembling legs. Still others, one on either side, were guardians of my arms and pinned them back and away. And one brute more, his hand sunk into my hair, pulled back against the headboard, while his other grasped my lower jaw and chin and pressed it hard. Thus was I pinioned and made to sit immobile and compressed during the whole of the unspeakable business.

What kind of man becomes a surgeon? More assassin than healer! One who responds with a bestial joy to the splitting of innocent flesh, whose own blood leaps and froths at the spillage of another's. Yet all is garbed in the grim respectability of the Professor, masked in the peculiarly deadly and monotonous language of the Scientist.

"Thus and thus to freshen the edges of the skin."

"Thus to cut the cartilage," he instructed in his fearsome language.

I screamed as the knife entered my face.

I marvel again and again that this man and I use the same words, the same mode of speech, so alien is he to my spirit. Envision him in his great black hat, a pointed beard resting like a pigeon on the gaudy white ruff of his collar; his heavy black robes trimmed with sable; and on two each of the fingers of both hands, rings, at least one of amethyst, the other of lapis lazuli, and a ruby which glittered close to my eyes and bit into my cheek during the manipulation.

Above and about the Enactment lounged the visitors as at a gallery. Behind fans and kerchiefs they bent and whispered, smiling, if you can imagine it, then staring fixedly, their lips parted, a high color in their cheeks, as the knife sliced me and the bloody torrent rained from my lips and chin. One is Tagliacozzi's mistress, of great and elegant fanciness, in whom it is said the blood lust is so great that only a daily such slaking as my ordeal suffices to keep her from frenzied rampaging through the populace. I shall not attempt to describe the hot pricking, the throbbing savage rendings which reverberated through my body from that central point. Jesus Christ, dear Saviour, my agony is beyond any imagining!

Next the slave, Virax, is seized and his arms fixed most sternly. A long strip of flesh at the upper inner portion of his arm is raised. It remains attached at one end. During all of this endeavor the slave makes no outcry or sound, but stands silent, even defiant. It is further proof that these low fellows have no feeling in them and, though Christians, are but Barnyard Beasts. Their thick insensitive flesh is made for beatings and hard labor, nor are they enriched by any of the sensory raptures which are a necessity to us. The slave's arm, now so prepared, is then brought to suspend across my face and the described flap of tissue is stitched to my nose stump in the costliest way. One would have thought that even Virax's heart would be moved by my screams, but no, the animal stood, even watched, without a mote of expressiveness. Oh, how we are made to pay for our Gentility! Then round and round with cords and cloths we are bound, I and Virax, joined into a single pain-racked creature with two heads, the one lowering and pouting grudgingly above the other, whose piteous attitude is such that my own poor brow is buried with grotesque intimacy into the axillary parts of my detested partner, and my lips against his flesh are pressed in a most reluctant kiss.

So have we remained these three weeks, and what a Hell is mine! I have lain with him, listened to his waters, suffered his bowels, endured the belching and snoring which he trumpets into my defenseless ear. To think that from this lump of filth is to be carved my own Dear Nose. Time and again have I wept, implored, cursed, even pinched and dug him in the back with my hands, but to no avail; he returns me no consideration, no single kindness. More than once have I regretted the adventure which has entwined our eight extremities in this loathsome contortion. I pray God will not punish me further for my vanity. How much can I bear? And how I yearn for the Detachment. The dreaded perpetrator, Tagliacozzi, comes each day. For fifteen days and nights more will I be Virax's appendage and he mine. The area of joining has begun to smell. Of this I complained most bitterly to Tagliacozzi, who in a most casual and deplorable tone reassured me that the advent of sepsis was not unexpected, and even praiseworthy.

I can write no more. The awkward position in which I must pen this letter strains me beyond endurance. I kiss your hands.

In friendship,
BARTOLOMEO VINCENZI

A second letter followed by seven days its predecessor:

April 22, 1584

Your Serene Eminence,

It is not myth that the excrescences of the lower classes are fouler by far than the tidy leavings of the highborn. These latter are shaped and turned almost in our likenesses, and are sweetly redolent as of old parchment. But these, oh these, sir, Virax among them, their runnings and flatulence would nauseate a wolf. Is it any wonder, then, that there is among the Aristocracy a certain subtle, shall I say, reluctance, or better still, regret, to part with that which, harbored by our bodies, coated by our essences, has taken on in some small and secret way the character of our very selves? Thrust from the shrine of their creation, with a sweet ambivalence, they are not wholly unlike the relics of saints, to be encased in silver boxes, on satin laid, for everlasting veneration by the rabble. Think if you will (but for a moment only, lest you be overcome) of me, rooted as I am to the coarsest of beings, my own gentle flesh burrowing into his in a coupling scarcely to be imagined, our adjacent orifices discharging side by side, the One decorous, reticent, totally inoffensive, the Other exploding in unlicensed effrontery, with such a miasma of fumes, such a cannonade, as to offend the beasts of the field, as I have noted above.

Enough, I can write no more.

Your brother-in-law,
BARTOLOMEO VINCENZI

Six weeks after the surgery, he writes:

June 2, 1584

Your Revered Eminence,

At last, at last, the day has come. We are led to the surgery, and again I sit upon the dais with Virax behind me in the position of our original joining. Here again is Tagliacozzi—ponderous, bulky, secretive, savoring. I am astonished to find his hand so small and delicate, with a hue pale and milky, like the unused hand of a cloistered nun. Once again

45

we are seated and held by the knaves. The blade is raised. With heart pumped dry, I wait for the pain, but to my amazement I feel none. The disjunction is quickly completed and such is my joy to see the hated arm of Virax secede from myself that I involuntarily struggle to rise and turn in my new freedom. Only the steely grip of the restrainers prevents me. I have survived! Such an ecstasy is mine as Saint Theresa must have enjoyed in her Holy Communion. Tagliacozzi cuts, presses, shapes, and fashions the tubelike appendage I now wear. I am indifferent to the procedure, and equally to his whore, who bends from the gallery to peer shamelessly at my blood and open flesh, and to expose the tops of her nipples. Gracefulness will be mine, all the more elaborate and delectable for having passed through the Flames of Hell. To be fully Nosed, accoutered! I long for you to see me in my nascent splendor. I am your affectionate servitor,

BARTOLOMEO VINCENZI

This on the day prior to our departure from Bologna:

June 24, 1584

Your Revered Eminence,

Two thousand scudi! For what? It is monstrous. The greed of Tagliacozzi is beyond belief. Tomorrow I depart the Pirate's Lair and well away I shall be. Two thousand scudi indeed! It is the ransom of a princeling. With what a cool and ivory countenance he informed me of his fee, stating that is the price for a high Roman, and had I wished something less grand, say a "turned-up" or a bulbous, I should have so expressed myself prior to the Reconstruction. Nevertheless I paid it, and it will doubtless amuse you to know that with characteristic grandness I threw a hundred scudi more upon the desk, "to defray any incidental expenses." This spoken with all the hauteur at my command.

But it is beautiful! It smells, it twitches, it dilates, it contracts—in short, it is a nose! A fine narrow arch so like unto the first of my olfactory appendages as to be proud in the comparison. The stench of alley buckets will set me sniffing greedily until, discovered, I shall sidle away in shame to some new aroma. Let me wine and attars, meats and bakery inhale and grow faint in the new doing. It is a rebirth, a renascence. Oh, what shall I not do with my new nose!

46

This upon our return to Mantua:

July 12, 1584

Your Revered Eminence,

On the triumph of my return to Mantua, may I beg the indulgence of your Gracious Eminence to wax rhapsodic. I, without the slightest tendency to overstate a simple fact, with an abhorrence of the flowery perversion of the vocabulary, and with a controlled and dignified mannerism befitting our station, must nevertheless inform you of the spectacular details of my arrival. Word of my coming had encouraged the lickerish crowd to fill the streets in an unbroken line on either side, their hard little eyes glinting. How they would have loved to laugh at my disfigurement, to rejoice at my folly and failure. I confess that I yielded to the Temptress Herself at that moment, and ordering the carriage to halt, stepped from it to the street and, head held high, barefaced, I thrust between the rows, thrilling to the waves of admiration which passed across them like an audible wind through a grassy field. Straightaway to the cathedral did I go, there to have the blessing of the priest on my new nose. This he did with all due ceremony. The feasts, the ovations, the toasts were sumptuous, to which I, in all generosity, invited the townsfolk, regardless of station or justification.

Your brother-in-law,
BARTOLOMEO VINCENZI

On January 4, 1585, Bartolomeo again wrote to the Cardinal:

Tagliacozzi has done well, the bandit. But two thousand scudi! Yet I shall not brood upon this inordinate display of greed. It is to Heaven that I shall leave the distasteful task of settling with a villain who coldly and brazenly fills his cellars with the gold born of misery and wretchedness. Is it not infamous, Your Eminence, that in this day of Enlightenment we have not regulated Medicine to the needs of the sick, given it into the hands of men whose sole interest is the dispersion of Health and Well-Being? I cannot but mourn the passage of this Noble Pursuit into the hands of purveyors and predators, among whom I regretfully include the surgeon Tagliacozzi.

One thought only rankles, lies coiled in my bosom like an asp, poisons the sweetness of my new life, and which as God is in Heaven I cannot dislodge: its name is Virax. Oh, how the thought of this man

47

inflames me, renders me mad with hatred and the Need for Revenge! No wild mother bear, shambling about the corpses of her slain cubs, slathering with rage, compares to me in my Absolute Requirement for Virax's death. That a creature such as he should walk this earth, free and willful, masquerading as a human being, and with the filthy triumph in his heart, the triumph of having once joined to my flesh, lain with me, spilled upon me, insulted me with his nearness, nay, his indispensability, this I cannot longer and will not, I vow it, endure. Even now my men are dispatched to the village of his residence, where he sits in the taverns and nightly lowers his sleeves to show the gawking drunkards the scar by which he enslaved me, a noble Lord such as yourself! It is not solely, I assure you, for my own dignity and self-respect that he must be terminated. He is a blatant insult to our entire Class. It is not to be countenanced, and I, Bartolomeo Vincenzi of Mantua, will be the protector of Our Honor. Virax is to be seized, told briefly the source of his doom, and dispatched with three piercings of his heart. If no unforeseen circumstance has caused a delay in their accomplishment (and I shall brook none), even now the wretch is confronted with my steel. I must go now. Forgive me this abrupt closing, Your Eminence. I am suddenly unwell. My nose gives me pain.

Bartolomeo

Even as my hand was tracing the flourish of his signature, my heart pounded with fear. This was indeed the last limit of reason. My master had lurched into madness! Terrified of his wrath, I spoke.

"Forgive me, master. You must not do this thing, I implore you! Beware the soul of Virax, lest it undo you! Take what is but lent. . . ."

Mindless, I continued to speak.

"Does not the soul hold sway over all parts, even those severed or separated? Master, I myself stood in witness at the burial of Ponchiello's left leg. Prayers were said, the priest gave last rites. Ponchiello's wife wept measures of tears over the corpselet. Master, if . . ."

"Sheathe your tongue," he muttered, "or you shall not long have it."

As I watched, he rose to his feet, wonder growing in his eyes, then horror. He flung his hands to his face and staggered to my desk. There he stood, a pitiable sight, rocking to and fro in a crouching stance.

"What is it, master? You are ill!"

At that moment there was a small movement on his face, as though something had slipped or given. Then a sound as of a soft object striking the paper on which I had been writing.

I stared down at the black thing that lay there. One could still see the refinement in the curve of its nostrils.

Minor Surgery

What am I doing here? he thought. This is crazy. I don't want to do it. I should get up and leave—now, while there's still time. Why did I listen to her?

But Nathan stayed.

"This will be just a little pinprick and a slight burning for a minute. You won't feel anything after that. Ready? Here goes."

Nathan felt the sting of the needle, a moment of heat, then nothing.

"Good boy," said the voice behind the mask. The eyes looked approvingly at him.

Get up, get up, run, quick, he thought. But Nathan stayed. He looked downward as far as he could, so as to watch the operation. He could see only the brown rubber-gloved hand, the handles of the clamps and scalpel. He lay still, stopped trying to see, and closed his eyes.

It was just a month ago that he lay on his back, playing who would blink first with the moon. The lecherous tide fingered and licked his heels in a kind of foreplay of the swim he was intending to take. From the periphery of his stare he could see a disembodied hand moving confidently up his arm, stuffing itself greedily with the muscles of his chest, playing with the nipple, then moving across his center. Suddenly it stopped and flung itself away as though scalded.

"Why don't you get rid of it, Nathan?"

With effort, he remained motionless, fighting off the urgent need to blink, then abruptly surrendered to the moon and closed his eyes.

"What?" He rolled onto his stomach.

"Have it removed. It's not as though it would take a big operation. I'm sure it wouldn't be very painful, and then only for a short time."

"Do you know the definition of a 'minor operation,' Sheila? It's one that's done on somebody else."

"For me, Nathan?" The voice was soft, persuasive.

"Why?"

"I hate it. It's so ugly, I don't want to touch it. And any time I try to avoid it, there it is, the furry soft disgusting thing."

He had risen to a kneeling position and pulled his shirt on over his head.

"There. That better?"

"No. It's there and I know it. I can almost see it through your shirt. It's—it's pink and buttery and squat."

"You really couldn't be worrying too much about it, Sheila."

"Don't get sensitive, please, Nat. It isn't that. It's repulsive to me. Can't you do it for me? To satisfy me? I love you."

"All right," he whispered at last. He rose as he said it and turned to step into the water.

"All right?" she asked quickly. "Did you say 'all right'? You will? Oh, Nathan, thank you, my darling. When, when?" She knelt in front of him, her face buried in his abdomen, her arms encircling his waist. With a steady, meaningful pull she drew him to his knees and down on all fours. In a sudden movement, she slithered beneath him and wrapped her arms about his neck. Her legs encircled his body as she pulled herself up to him from the sand, clinging like a suckling pig, all but their chests touching.

His mother had called it his strawberry. It was about that size, pink in color, although deepening to a red when he laughed or

51

cried. The surface was smooth, with a little lawn of short pale velvety hair. She hadn't minded looking at it, would even formally examine it from time to time, remarking:

"Well, now, Nathan, I do believe your strawberry is shrinking. It certainly looks paler to me today."

It never did shrink, and in fact grew as he grew, so that it always occupied the same percentage of his body surface. After a while his mother stopped examining it and giving her homely progress reports. Once he had asked her, "Why do I have this, Mother?"

"Your strawberry, Nat? That's because you're special. It means you're going to be somebody, yes you are."

He remembered (or did someone tell him?) how, when he was two years old, he had stood, delighted, before the mirror, having found the birthmark with a finger, looking from flesh to glass, then back again. He was fascinated by it. He would find his hand wandering to that spot on his chest, burrowing beneath his shirt. At night in his bed, it was soothing to touch it; there was a reassurance in it, as though, by virtue of its being extra, added on, he could focus on it, as a boat upon its anchor, a kite upon its string. So long as he knew it was there he was all right, moored. Even today, he would fall asleep touching it, as though it were a button which, pressed, sent beams of sleep penetrating his body.

At sixteen, he dreamed of a voluptuous woman who, among other things, would lick the mole and bite it softly with her small even teeth, picking at the small folds and letting them drop back from her lips. She would have to be a prostitute. No nice girl would do it. He would pay her a fortune, but it would be worth it, and each time she did it, he would go mad for days at a time, during which he would experience oracular visions of stunning importance.

Sheila had come with him to the doctor's office and was waiting in the outer room to take him home. "I know you're doing it just for me. I'm so terribly grateful. As soon as you're through I'll drive you home and we'll rest there together, play some records. You can take a nap."

"All right, Sheila, it's coming off. Let's not talk about it anymore."

"You won't hate me afterwards, will you? Please don't resent me. It's because I love you so, I want you to be perfect, and now you will be."

He rose at the nurse's call. There was a firm squeeze of his hand from Sheila. "Be brave, darling."

"There, it's done," said the muffled mouth. "It wasn't so bad, was it?"

Nathan knew that he was fundamentally altered. It was as though he had become an adjunct to the birthmark, and now that it lay some distance from him, he was bereft in some elemental way. He raised his head to see it lying on a square of white gauze, stained with a corona of blood. It glowed like a jewel.

Oh, God, he thought. At that moment, he wanted only one thing: He wanted it back. He felt that his head had also been injected with Novocaine. He tried to think of something, anything, but like a numb lip his brain refused to move. He lay there stiff and lumpy, knowing that when he did start to think, it would come out like a lopsided smile. He watched the doctor grasp it with a forceps, hold it briefly to the light, then shake it into a small bottle of formaldehyde. The birthmark resisted stickily, and in the end the doctor pushed it from the end of his forceps with a rubber-gloved finger. It swam jerkily around in the jar, as though measuring its tiny grave, and sank joylessly to the bottom and lay still.

"Here. Inhale this." The doctor broke a pellet in his fingers and held it under Nathan's nose. "Take deep breaths and it will pass soon. Don't worry about it."

Acrid fumes bit him sharply. He coughed and turned away,

then sat up and swung his legs over the side.

"Are you all right? You're still pale. Better stay a while longer."

The nurse was mechanically concerned. He walked from the operating room and into the crowded waiting room. Sheila stood as soon as he appeared and linked her arm in his. "It wasn't too bad, was it, darling?"

Nathan looked at her as though for the first time. His arm freed itself from her grasp, rose, and swung dryly with a crackling sound and great force across the side of her head. The smile broke off her face and crashed to the floor. Its splinters flew among the startled patients.

The Fur Baby

To look at her you would have thought she had been dug out of the ice, one of those prehistoric creatures that freezes alive in a crevice and a million years later thaws and lumbers off, old as the planet, and with an eon's thoughts having drifted like a sky across its brain.

Luna knew they hated having her around, could scarcely wait for her to die. So she stayed upstairs in her room and hadn't come down for three years, not even for meals.

"What if you get sick and need the doctor?" asked Joe. "What then? It'd look just fine for us to have you up there sick and not take you to the doctor." But she had already decided that if that happened, she'd either get better or she wouldn't, and that was all there was to it. But she wouldn't go downstairs.

Joe had the most irritating voice of any man she knew. There was a moistness to it as though there were bubbles in his throat through which the words slowly rose like the gases in stagnant water. Even as a child he had sounded that way and she was forever telling him to please clear his throat, but even when he did it didn't help, and she found herself clearing her own throat whenever he was talking.

Also he was bald. And that, God forgive her, was one thing she found ugly. Luna knew it wasn't anything he could help, but still every time she saw him, all she could look at was that yellow pie of a scalp shedding what looked like silverfish onto his shoulders. God forgive me, she thought, my own flesh and blood. After a while Joe had stopped persuading her to come down. She knew all along that he didn't really want her to, was just acting righteous, the priss. Stella was really the only one who ever came up to her room and then only with the tray. She didn't even bother to talk anymore since Luna like as not wouldn't answer. She chose to speak rarely these days. For one thing she didn't like the way her voice sounded—an old lady's quaver. It bothered her to hear it and realize it was hers. In fact it bothered her almost as much as Joe's did. But the other reason for not answering Stella was because there wasn't anything she could say, not even "Good morning," without being so false she'd rather die. After a while the silence had become an addiction from which she derived comfort, like cigarettes or whiskey. It gradually became just as hard to break and in time she didn't bother to try.

Stella was used to being careful. She and Joe had been child-hood sweethearts, although that wasn't really the name for it. They had each just always been around the other, so that when they finally did get married, Stella was twenty-eight; it was like putting on an old pair of slippers, and hardly anyone noticed. And Luna didn't know but she was almost certain that it wasn't good for them to have spent all that time together before they got married, warily circling each other's bodies for fifteen years, until finally when it was all right and legal and everything, they seemed startled by the whole idea of it, and whether they didn't or couldn't or what, they certainly acted mighty cold. Luna had never seen them touch except once accidentally when they bumped, each recoiling as though the other were a live wire. They didn't have any children. Whether it was instead, or just naturally, they loved things and went about saving them like squirrels. The house was stuffed with things. Nothing worth anything, mind you, but a lifetime of string and rubber bands, bottles, what living people would consider trash.

Luna could hardly bear to look at Stella. It was her eyes, surmounted as they were by thin penciled chevrons, although why she would ever want to call attention to those eyes Luna couldn't fathom. Dull and sessile as underwater plants, they sat dead center until washed listlessly from side to side by some slow current of thought. Beneath them the black really started, deepening in circles and running halfway down her cheeks. They looked for all the world like a pair of black stockings hanging on a clothesline.

So she would just tap on the door with her foot, come in, set the tray down, pick up the one from the previous meal, and go back out. But there wasn't anything they could do. It was her house, and she had willed it to Stella and Joe just to make sure that they stayed around and kept interested in her. Somehow she knew that they'd stay if they knew they'd get the house and all. Corruption, she thought, and although she didn't smile, the faint desire was there as she thought of how she lived, a fierce old weed that grows best in the meanest place.

One time the door had not been closed tight, and she had heard Stella's voice rising in hysteria. "I hate her, hate her, hate her! I can't stand it anymore!" Then she heard Joe gargling to her, soothing her, making it all better. Joe hated her, too, but he couldn't have dispossessed his own mother, not in Ellenville, and stay here. Not with the whole town watching, he couldn't. They would just have to wait and endure like everyone else, like me, she thought.

It was like wings unfolding, the way she brushed the open pages of the magazine with her sleeves. From her lap the gaze was fierce, unblinking, on the verge of rage even, but with hard rays of intelligence. They were like sisters, the eagle on the page, all horn and talon, and the one in the chair, beaked as well and proud, with the meditation of the nest upon her.

She let the magazine slide from her lap, and with her right hand pushed the left sleeve of her sweater up. Folding her arm across her chest, she studied the mole just above the elbow. It was dark brown, the size of a quarter, and covered with a lawn of dark hair. There was a certain strength to it, emphasized by the pale skin that hung in atrophic folds around it.

They had all said that she had given it to him from her genes, and that the mole on her arm was where her seed was, and when she had conceived, it swept all through the baby's cells and he was born with it all over his body except for a spot the size of a quarter on his left thigh, which was pink and smooth. Even now the voices came to her, and when she heard them all say "God" and "Jesus" and "Holy Christ," had raised her head to peer between her open upslung thighs, to peer at what slid from her, brown and furry, and thought it was a beast, a cub. "It looks like a monkey," she had said, and they hadn't said a word and that was how she knew.

"We can't show it to her. My God ugh it's horrible monster never saw anything like it I feel sick worst put her to sleep put it to sleep." The voices reached her through the billowing nausea of gas, the words ringing louder and louder in her ears even as their meaning withdrew from her, out of reach, irretrievable.

"Let me see," she whispered.

"Not now."

"Yes. Let me see."

"Not now."

"When?"

"Later."

"Oh," she heard herself moan.

"Hairy mole," said the doctor. "Nothing to do. Entire body covered."

She remembered that later when the nurse brought him to her and laid him in her arms, wrapped in a blanket except for his face, in which the tiny wet pebbles of his eyes glittered and only the tips of the ears poked through the fur.

"I want to see it all," she said.

58

"All right, if you want to," said the nurse, and unwrapped it, and Luna looked for a long time at the hands and feet, which were like paws, and the chest and abdomen, still matted with the moisture of birth.

"What's that?" she asked, pointing to a pink smooth spot on the front of one thigh. It was about the size of a quarter.

"That's the only place it isn't. The only normal skin he's got."

That spoils it, thought Luna. "He's not perfect," she said sadly.

"These things happen, honey. Don't decide now. Give yourself a chance to think it over, and if you do decide we'll send him to a place where he'll get the best. Nothing but the best."

Luna stared down at the creature which if it had been an animal would have been adorable, she thought. She studied the patterns of shine in the fur and for the first time touched his velvet with the backs of her fingers. What seized her then was more impulse than intention, and raising him up she laid her cheek against his chest, holding herself still, listening to his— but really to her own—heart, to learn what she was, what she felt, for she still did not know. The faint tickle of his hair, and the small quick breaths that rose and fell against her face, began to tell her . . . that I love, she thought, need, must, and that whatever comes, at least for this time and instant, there is love.

She had thought then in the beginning, Well, at least he's not blind, with flat pumpkin-seed eyes. Not those bright little peepers of his darting this way and that and taking it all in. He sees everything there is to see. It's just . . . and here she had grown quiet and very tired all at once. He won't share it with anyone. He'll see all right but there won't be anyone to give it out to and get it back. But that was all right, too, because . . . neither do I, she thought.

Much later when the trouble began she couldn't stop wishing that somehow they could meld again so that the next time around one of them could have it all and that it would be her,

Luna, that had all the fur instead of one little spot, and that he could be like everyone else. Once she dreamed that the mole was a garment and she could slip it off his body and draw it onto her own, stretching it out to fit. But it wasn't and she couldn't and afterward she forced herself to be gay, and played with him for hours.

She had thought she loved that man in Portland. Adam Thoms was straight and had a low sweet voice, and when he knelt and pressed his lips against her knee it made a whirring like wings that rose and hovered somewhere in a place that had always been still, like a pond. That's what it was like and she really thought she loved him. Never saw him after that, after that first month, but when she had begun to show, Luna went to a hospital clinic there in Portland where nobody knew her. She kept going back until she had the baby, and it was the hardest thing she had ever done. It was like an exorcism, as though what it was really for was to get rid of that man's stuff, his presence that he had left in her, but that it had gotten so far in that the only way to get rid of it was to travel to Hell and back, which she did, she did, and when it was over, and when all her flesh, which had been cut into strips and peeled off her bones, had been put back, and she was whole again, well, then she was purified.

It must have been the sound of its heart going *lubdup lubdup* against her ear, or when she heard it crying in a human way, that she decided to keep it. Later, though, they had all said no and how can you and better not to. But she had secretly named him Poem, and not Lewis, which she called him, and after that could not, even if she had wanted to, which she definitely did not. Poem for a lot of reasons, one because it was the most beautiful word and she owed that to him, and also because he was what she had made and it told all about her the way a poem does, and she felt she owed it to herself after all that she had been through.

For a long time it was all right because she was able to work and keep them both but when he got to be a year and a half old and started to walk, he'd wander off and she couldn't hide him anymore and nobody wanted him around, and no matter how often she went and got him and brought him back and hugged and kissed him and wrapped him about, Poem had to get out, and she knew it would be bad because she had seen the other children laughing and scared and she knew that wasn't safe, for people to be laughing and scared, and one day she came home to find him lying in the alley in back of the yard with a dent in his forehead and blood matting his lovely fur, and he was dead.

The next year she had married and then there was Joe, but it wasn't the same and nothing was special anymore like he was, like Poem. She had never told a word of it to anyone and wouldn't either, even though they vexed her by being so superior and haughty, when in fact none of them had ever had such a thing, anything special, happen to *them*.

Korea

She was the tallest Korean woman he had ever seen. Her face was frozen in an expression of permanent terror, as manifested in the perilous bulging of the eyes; so proptosed were they, in fact, as to reveal vast naked expanses of the white globes, upon the apices of which the pupils perched, pathetically small by comparison. Sloane had an involuntary urge to run toward her, basin in hand, for fear that one or both would momentarily be popped from their socket by the slightest intake of breath. Her mouth, drawn back and fixed in a grin, presented the maximum orifice for intake of air. Despite this and the wildly flaring nostrils, she gasped rapidly and shallowly, like a spent runner who fights to pay the debt of oxygen borrowed from heart and brain.

He watched Yoon interviewing them, taking the history. At one point the man stepped forward and unpinned the cloth around her neck. Yoon sucked in his breath as the woman's throat was bared. Sloane repressed the desire to do the same. Filling the space between chin and breastbone, and forcing the head back, was an enormous rounded eminence the size of a grapefruit. More than anything, she resembled a startled blowfish. Sloane rose and approached her.

"How long has she had this?"

"Five years, Sir Doc. Only twenty days now, all of a sudden get too big." He cupped his hands.

"Does she have pain?"

Yoon spoke, and the woman answered in what to Sloane was the product of no human larynx. Shrilling through that dry doorway was a metallic whine, all of the same single note, not bearing the slightest inflection or accent, as if such a luxury would tax beyond renewal whatever fragile ghostly reeds vibrated in her throat.

"No, sir, no pain. Only cannot breathe. No can swarrow. No can rie down, only stand up or sit down."

"How did they get here? Where do they live?"

"He shay walk twenty miles, two days, to see ouisa. Sir Doc, he shay prease can fix him wife? Pretty soon die."

Sloane led her to a chair and began to outline the tumor with his fingertips. Hopefully he tapped the surface, waiting for the returning vibratory wave which would indicate fluid. Fluid could be withdrawn through a needle to diminish the size of the mass, and make surgery feasible. There was none. Sloane had never seen such a goiter. There was no place to send her. What if there was bleeding from high and behind it, where he could not see to control it? What if she could not tolerate the local anesthetic? He had no means to put her to sleep. It would have to be Novocaine, with her wide awake. In the end he simply dared himself to do it.

"Tell her I'll take it out," he said to Yoon. "Tomorrow morning."

The message was transmitted; the woman, unable to bow, pressed her palms together in gratitude, her expression unchanged. Her husband retreated to the door and out the dispensary, to wait in the road by the village until the next day.

By the time Sloane had finished his surgical residency, the early thirst for pathology had already been slaked. It was normalcy he craved, normalcy with its clean lines and rounded glistening eminences, the unclouded lens, the white whipslide of a tendon, the airy comb of the lung, elastic, continually re-

63

freshed. Still, it was in the ricochet from disease that he was able, privileged, he thought, to see the sad beauty of man, tangentially, on the rebound, and he found himself more and more—then always—waiting, receptive, for that special little moment of revelation when that which he thought most akin to classic nobility would flare like a dying star.

That night Sloane did not sleep. He spent an hour reviewing the surgery of the thyroid gland; fixed in his mind the exact location of the superior and inferior thyroid arteries, the middle thyroid vein, the recurrent laryngeal nerve. Toward morning he could see an artery torn and spurting, hear the swish of blood from it, knew that it was out of sight, out of reach.

At 7:30 A.M. she was lying on the table, grinning still at the ceiling. She was bare to the waist, and a rolled blanket had been thrust transversely beneath her upper back so that her head fell back and rested on the table, and the neck presented the tumor to best advantage. For twenty minutes he scrubbed her neck, chest, and chin with warm soapy water, while the instruments were soaked in alcohol and laid out. He could see the mass pulsating slightly with her heartbeat, as ominous as a time bomb awaiting detonation. Alcohol was rubbed into her skin and drapes were laid about the neck. One towel was loosely dropped over her face.

"Jang, tell her she's going to feel a needle."

The tripartite conversation began. He had become so used to speaking through an intermediary that often he was surprised to receive a direct and immediate answer.

"Now another. Pretty soon it will be all numb. I know it burns now." (God help me, let me get it out.) "All right, tell her she can breathe just fine, and if she can't, if she needs more air, to raise her left hand off the table a little and I'll pick up the towel." (No blood transfusions, no oxygen, no nothing.) "Here we go. Knife."

64

From earlobe to earlobe. He'd need all the room he could get.

"Clamps. Come on, get in here, help clamp. Lightly, lightly, don't press. It doesn't take much." (Oh, God, these boys don't know anything. I've trusted them too much. But look how scared they are right now, and I'm scolding. We're all scared; she least of all, I think. Isn't that remarkable?)

Next he dissected the skin and overlying tissues off the surface of the tumor, upward and down as far as he could. It's hurting! He saw, out of the corner of his eye, the left hand stir and falter into the air, just an inch, then, gathering courage, it dropped back.

"Novocaine! Tell her it'll be better in a minute. There. O.K., retractors. Hold them like this. No, goddamn it, just so. Do as I say." (Goddamn these ignorant gooks. Forgive me.)

The last thin layer of covering was stripped from the surface of the tumor and it bulged nakedly, throbbing, tense with blood. It was purple, crisscrossed with interlacing veins and arteries. With his index finger he began to break up the filmy adhesions between its surface and the adjacent structures. With infinite care he swept his finger to and fro, each time a bit further. Instantly the wound filled with blood, obscuring the operative field.

"Watch out! Clamp! Clamp! Wipe! Wipe! O.K. I've got it. Suture."

He controlled the torn vessel with pressure from his finger. Now, still holding it, he passed a stitch into the mass beneath his finger, then again. When he removed his finger the lake of blood instantly reappeared. He tied the first knot, then threw down the second and third, and wiped the blood away.

"That's got it. Good. Now let's go."

That first drenching lowered him into the battle, somehow calmed him. He might be able to do it again now, if he had to. Now the entire front of the tumor was cleared and he worked around to the sides, peeling away strands of muscle, clamping, ligating, dividing vessels.

"Novocaine."

Giving the anesthetic was an interlude in the implacable advance of the operation. He allowed himself to relax for the time. It was something to do that carried no danger. He was certain that she enjoyed the respite as much as he.

One by one he located and surrounded the great vessels of the thyroid, passing silk threads beneath them, tying his heart down with each knot. Both superior vessels, then the inferior two. Now it's done. Start peeling out.

"Watch for the parathyroids. Mustn't take it all. Leave a bit. Boy, look at that trachea." The cartilage rings and the windpipe were compressed, eroded. "No wonder she couldn't breathe. Here we go. One more snip. It's out."

The slippery purple ball lay in his hands. He cradled it for a moment like the heart of a saint, then set it in a basin.

"Let's wash this out and get out of this neck. Saline, sutures. Put a heavy compression dressing on, not too tight or she'll choke. All done, mama-san. Good brave girl." He squeezed her hand.

A week later when they left, she had shrunken somehow, was indistinguishable from all the other Korean women, but Sloane remembered her as she had been, an empress, tall and stiff and tortured, grinning as she was led about.

Sloane was lancing an abscess when it happened. He saw his hand, holding the scalpel, trembling. At first finely, but as he watched it grew into a coarser movement, a shaking no longer even and regular but occasionally flying into a widely swinging jerk. He backed off from the bristling red mound in the middle of the man's back.

"Shut that door!" he called out. "It's colder than hell in here."

But the man, naked to the waist, wasn't shivering.

"It is shut, Sir Doc," came the reply.

Take care of yourself, Sloane, he whispered, you're tired. But this is just an abscess. Simple, no danger. Calm down.

He forced himself to relax, taking deep breaths and pushing them slowly out. He was dismayed to feel even his breath quivering, moving in and out in short staccato bursts.

He advanced again upon the abscess. Once more his right hand disobeyed his brain, discharging its movement in a senseless epileptiform manner. He grasped it with his other hand, pressing firmly, and pushed the quivering blade to the apex of the mound. At the last moment it veered crazily off center and stabbed a good half inch to the side of the lesion. A stripe of useless red appeared where it had struck.

He felt heat searing his face and the collar of his shirt was already uncomfortably damp. Again he steeled the muscles of his arms, and aimed the vibrating blade toward the patient. He was frightened, felt threatened. With his whole strength and control he moved ahead. He had no idea, by this time, where the capricious knife would choose to land. At the last instant a third hand, brown, cool, hard, swam into his field of vision and closed upon his two. In an instant he felt steadier, less paroxysmal. He let the hand grip his and take control. Relaxing into passivity, he gave up to this new force. The scalpel drove straight to the mark, stabbed, then cut. A line of blood, then a velvety wave of greenish-white pus erupted from the wound in a small geyser, until, its pressure spent, it settled down into a steadily moving stream across the man's back.

He looked up at Jang and murmured tremulously:

"P-pack it with g-gauze when it stops."

He stood there helplessly as Jang pried his rigid fingers from the knife handle.

"Sir Doc sick! Shaky! Too hot sick! Feber! Too bad sick! No can do sick call."

Sloane felt himself growing sick, as though Jang's words had freed his illness to manifest itself, or had at least brought it to the surface of his awareness. Jang's face was a mask of anxiety and gloom.

"We go bed now, Sir Doc." He put his arm around Sloane, tucking his hand under the armpit and lifting. "Ah, tsk tsk tsk. Sir Doc number ten sick."

He helped him to a cot in the dispensary and began removing his clothes. Sloane's entire body shook violently, the metal cot rattling on the floor like a snare drum. Weakness, profound, deep as a well, flooded him and he gave up all hope of self-control. Tears came to his eyes and rolled down his cheeks. He tried to talk but his lips seemed to have liquefied, and any attempt to speak caused them to flow into the most exaggerated shapes.

"Hoo, boy, temperature one hundred five," said Yoon reverently. "Too much sick. Maraddia. Give Tocshan chlorquin pills, mo'skoshi. Rub alcohol all over body. Pretty soon good, O.K., number one."

Sloane heard them discussing his illness and the treatment. Through the weakness and nausea he knew they were right. Malaria. He lapsed into delirium, giving in to the chill, feeling his flesh flinging itself helter-skelter on the cot. At one point Yoon and Jang, moving on either side, placed their arms across his body to keep him from flopping onto the floor.

"Stop! You're killing me!" he screamed. "You fucking gooks. I hate you and your fucking no-good country. Stop!" His voice raged, hoarse, desperate.

It was black, and he was lying in the shallows. Cold green waves slapped him back and forth, slapping his flesh into frozen weeds. Along came rats on the land and fish in the sea, and between the two they tore him leaf and stem to insignificant vegetation.

For hours the two Koreans rubbed his sizzling skin with alcohol, fanning the air to hasten evaporation and lower the temperature.

He was a naked neon corpse, twitching on and off.

"What it shay?"

"One hundred one. More better now. Can sreep."

Sloane heard their voices from deep within his head, round, hollow sounds, and fell asleep.

The next day he was weak, but the fever was only moderate. The chlorquin would take hold now. The boys were squatting in a corner and when he awoke they looked at him, smiling.

"Sir Doc talk prenty dirty rast night," said Yoon, and they both fell over onto the floor, laughing like hell.

They were walking home after a round of house calls in the village. Jang and Yoon were ahead with the bags. He watched them idly through half-closed lids. What babies they are! he thought. They walked side by side. Without warning one would step aside to get momentum, then go crashing into the other as if to knock him off the road. Sloane could hear them laughing and spitting, cursing. He relaxed and admitted his affection for these two. They were so damned innocent, he couldn't help it. Sometimes Sloane talked to them while they held sick call.

"Jang, these big white birds we see in the rice paddies, the ones with long legs. What do you call them?"

"They call hak, sir."

"Hak?" he would repeat.

They would invariably giggle when he attempted a Korean word, and soon he did it on purpose to make them silly.

"Hak, sir, he rive rong time. He ve-rrrr-y"—he drew the word out in a straining fashion—"old man; more than seventy year old. Korean people say hak he mean rong rife. If you catch hak you rive rong rifetime."

One day a little girl carried in a large bouquet of pink jindala. Yoon put it in a water bottle at Sloane's request and stood looking at it dreamily, lifting the petals on his fingertips with utmost gentleness.

"How long does the jindala last?" Sloane asked him.

Yoon shook his head rapidly, and Sloane was amazed to see tears in his eyes.

"Too very short. Couple days. Everybody say jindala is blood of young lovers spattered on mountains. Pretty soon sink in ground, dead."

He thought of these things as he followed them along the road. Suddenly Jang stopped and set down the satchel. Grabbing Yoon by one arm, he pointed down the road. He was excited, and in a second they both were, babbling to each other, smiling, their eyes lit, eager. He drew up.

"What is it?"

For the first time neither one answered him, nor did they take notice of his question. They seemed wholly absorbed, thrilled out of themselves by what they were watching.

"Dammit, answer me—what's going on over there?"

Yoon was the first to recover himself.

"Rock fight, Sir Doc."

"A rock fight?"

Yoon nodded eagerly.

"Korean peoples do, sometime. Is game. Rine up, throw rocks."

"At each other?"

They laughed then, nodding furiously.

"Why?"

Yoon shrugged and covered his mouth.

"That's crazy! They'll get hurt!"

More laughter, then a turning away again, as though pulled toward a custom stronger than their allegiance to him.

These goddamn people, he thought. Animals, that's what they are. A streak of cruelty just under their skin, hardly concealed. They were fine, fine, fine, but you must never forget who and what you're dealing with here.

Shielding his eyes from the sun, he looked down the road. About two hundred yards away, a cluster of people had organized into two groups on opposite sides of the road. They were separated by about fifty yards. They were not unlike players awaiting their turn. In one group Sloane saw a man whom he had treated at the dispensary some weeks ago. He had had an abscess of the leg which Sloane had drained. The man had suffered the ministrations with dignity, never expressing by the slightest sign that there was pain. And when it was done, he had bowed and smiled, backing to the door. Now he stood erect, swaggering, a billow to his pantaloons that had not been noticed before. In each hand he hefted a large rock of eminently throwable size. He was smiling, peppy, as he turned to laugh with his friends. Here on his home ground there was none of the deference that he had shown in the dispensary. There was only an easiness like that of the athlete who knows and loves his powers and longs to try them.

Sloane did not see the first throw. Or he might have and thought it was a bird that swooped low across the road. There was no flurry of rocks that followed. Only a slow, almost measured pace, a taking of time. Astonished, Sloane found himself aroused. With a mounting excitement he watched the rocks leaping across the road. A movement at his side brought him back to see Jang and Yoon loping toward the rock fighters, racing down the road, then at the last minute separating, each running to join a different team. In a moment he could see them lifting rocks, throwing them at each other, who a few minutes before were laughingly butting each other along the road. Now, from where he crouched behind a cover of trees, he could see the boys' faces, no longer laughing but wary, hostile, tight-lipped. Enemies.

There was a gracefulness to it, the rock fighting. Such a simple, pure, old act. Primitive man must have done it, just so. It must have been for that, just to pick up and throw a rock, that the thumb migrated from the line of the fingers and turned to oppose them, long ago. Then man stood up straight in order to throw better than he could on all fours. Rock throwing was fundamental activity. It went way back, and seeing it now, not for the hunt, nor for war, nor rage, jealousy or justice, but for joy, the elemental pleasure of an act as old as one's species, with which one feels so unified in body and intent, he thought, How is it that we have stopped throwing rocks? Why this embarrassment in doing man's own act? We have become too refined in our tastes, like certain perverts, and have lost our identity.

And Sloane slipped from behind the cover of trees and ran eagerly toward the rock fighters. He joined the group which he had counted as having fewer men and, stooping, picked up a rock. He leaned back on his right leg, his left leg raised straight ahead, and pulling his arm back to the limit he poured all his strength, concentrated, purified, into the rock, which flew straight, no trajectory but straight, into the line opposite. No sooner had it left his fingers than he bent to get another, and so did not see that it had struck with telling effect, and where eight had stood now seven remained, plus a muddy heap upon which two white rubber shoes had been tossed and from which a tongue of blood licked across a discarded Oriental mask.

The others were throwing now, firing one after the other. He could hear them thudding into the ground. Now and then a thud would be followed by a wail, Aie! Aie! and then a cheer from across the road.

Again and again his liberated arm threw thunderbolts, the clean sweat pouring down his shoulder blades, the smooth head of the humerus swiveling easily in its perfect socket. He heard the healthy animal grunt that came from his chest at the moment of discharge. It was a beautiful sound to him, shockingly strong and basic, a man sound, and he kept throwing until the others had run away. Even then he kept throwing for a while, and would have forever if Jang had not caught his arm.

"Sir Doc, all gone, no more rock fight! Yoon hurt bad."

Sloane stood panting, tousled, legs apart, staring at the rock in his hands, which after a few moments fell dully, unmusically to the ground. Jang led him across the road where Yoon lay; the others were gone, the wounded having been carried off by the rest. The boy lay on his back. Sloane's first rock had struck him in the face. Both lips had been split in two, the halves of the mouth falling away in a permanent purple grimace. The nose was a torn and twisted mound without visible nostrils. A star-shaped wound with its center just above the middle of the upper lip and radiating outward to the cheeks oozed blood in a folding, wavy-smooth sheet. It went to join the pile of black clot upon which Yoon's small, thin head rested. He looked as though someone had laid a poinsettia on his face. Sloane took the boy's hand and pressed it to his lips, all the while feeling himself clouding up inside with civilization, with mourning, having the sense that whatever blinding bright rays of light had momentarily shone down were diffused by the countless particles of dust stirred up along the sorry path of evolution.

They carried him into the ambulance. At the dispensary, Sloane washed and débrided the wounds and sutured them impeccably. It wasn't part of the game, and afterward he went to the outhouse and vomited long and eagerly, with all of his strength, until he was light and cold and empty.

A few weeks later, Yoon gave him an embarrassed smile, as though they had shared something secret, furtive, but pleasurable, like sex. When he smiled, Sloane could see the absence of teeth as a blackness between the crooked lips.

The ascent from the main gate to the dispensary was gradual enough, but Sloane noticed with what effort the Koreans strove to accomplish it. Tilting, swaying, sagging, the long line of stragglers managed the climb. Ordinary tasks seemed hopelessly difficult here, far beyond the stamina of the people, yet he saw them always and inexorably succeed, though not with the neat click and crunch of the West. They faltered, even fell, but moved on, pushed by the threat of numbers behind.

He leaned against the door of the Quonset hut that was the dispensary, feeling the weakness and the malaise of the patients penetrate his own body. He had awakened that morning to the familiar griping pain in his abdomen, the demands of foreign amoebae tunneling into his bowel. This and the sporadic rages of malarial fever combined to establish a kinship of disease between the Koreans and himself. It drove them together, a common ground of suffering for East and West. Perhaps therein lay the solution to the struggle of ideologies, he thought. Give both sides amoebiasis and malaria. There would be neither time nor energy for war. The only intercourse possible would be an occasional smile of sympathy and the fellowship of mutual suffering.

He watched two soldiers at the gate brusquely pushing away the next in line, holding them back while the gate was closed. He could not see, but had seen often enough to imagine, the little evidences of despair in those who had been turned away until the next day. They stood for minutes silently watching the fortunate ones who moved on up the road toward the doctor. Then they turned back toward the village, where they would hold themselves fragile and wilting through another day and night. They would come again the next day, unless that night a tiny weight dropped upon the scale and sank the balance. Each night there were such little deaths in the village.

The first patients had arrived and were squatting on the ground in clusters, waiting. A woman, thin as a finger save for her enormous abdomen, waddled into the examining room. She attempted to bow, basing her feet apart, supporting the great

74

belly with two hands underslinging its mass, and bent forward. One more millimeter would surely have changed her center of gravity, causing her to fall forward. He grasped the fleshless arm and steadied the wobbling frame, easing her onto the table.

"Ode appumnikka, mama-san?" he said. Where does it hurt?

Gasping for breath, mouth open, lips dry and fissured, the cadaverous face creased itself into an expression of pain and she pointed toward her abdomen. He undid the ties of her skirt and exposed her body. Instinctively her head turned away, showing the sheen of pulled black hair pierced at the back by a large silver needle. The hair seemed curiously young and vital, as misplaced on this body as a fern breaking from between dry desert boulders. He placed his hands on the tense abdomen and began the daily process of divination. Sloane could speak little Korean, and beyond the initiation of a physical examination and the most elementary of questions and comments, he was unable to communicate with his patients. It was like taking a box and shaking it to guess what lay inside. A gentle tap on the abdomen evoked a returning vibratory wave of fluid. The withdrawal of the fluid would decompress the abdomen and enable her to breathe easily. No cure, but a few weeks of relative comfort. She lay quietly as he cleansed the skin, infiltrated a local anesthetic, and punctured the abdominal wall with the hollow trocar. A gush of clear straw-colored fluid poured from the tube. Slowly the great tense swollen belly softened under his hand and shrank. Her breathing, at first grunting and shallow, came now more slowly, more amply. She sighed deeply, savoring the use of lungs that had been compressed, unfilled by air for months. She turned now to glance at him, forgetting and even forgiving the exposure of her body. Two gallons of fluid were removed and the abdomen was flat. He removed the trocar, covered the small wound with a dressing, and helped her to her feet. Smiling and babbling, she bowed now with grace and decorum, her head bent low to the ground. She would be back for the same procedure again and again. Sloane followed her easy departure with his eyes.

The next patient had already entered, a farmer with an open wound of the arm from which he brushed flies with a small fan. Over the bowing head Sloane saw the next patient in line, a girl perhaps twenty, her white skirt clean and stiff, the jacket trimmed with a thin strip of brown and gold brocade. She stood three-quarters turned away, gazing back above the crowd to the high distance beyond. There was something about the slender pillar of her neck. He bent over the man's arm. Deliberately he probed the wound, plumbing its depths, exploring the recesses. Then he cut away the necrotic infected tissue and applied antibiotic ointment and dressing.

"Come in three days," he said.

"Kommapsumnidda." Thank you.

The girl entered. She was pale and detached, avoiding his gaze.

"Ode appumnikka?" he asked.

Her wrist folded toward her chest. His days were so devoid of beauty that he had all but forgotten its presence, that there is a stirring in the body that is not painful. Her movement was wholly dignified. She seemed a lamp of milk glass which shed no rays but kept its cold small paleness within, dolorous and aloof.

"What is your name?"

"Shin Young Hae."

The syllables were breathed out and half drawn back within her.

"Nanungouisa. I am the doctor. I must examine your chest."

She loosened her skirt tie and sash and removed the small white jacket. He stood behind the childish shoulders and placed the stethoscope on her back. It seemed a violation, and for the first time in months he felt something different from the pity

76

which came to him many times each day. There was a difference here. He wanted not to hear, not to know, felt a longing to keep this girl outside the pale of disease, to keep her for himself. He listened and could hear only the blood beating in his own ears. The sudden ferocity of his desire frightened him. He withdrew his trembling hands from the girl, fearful that they might betray him. How preposterous, Sloane thought. Surely he must be feverish, the awakening of desire must be related to his weakness in some way.

"You may dress." The order was brusque. "You must come again tomorrow."

The girl stood up and bowed. At the nadir of the bow there was a turn of the head and he felt her eyes upon him for an instant, then the cool opalescence floated from the room. For the rest of the day Sloane lanced and drained, listened and percussed, cleaned and dressed. He finished and stood alone in the dispensary in the space where she had stood, where she had leaned, straining to feel her coolness with his hands.

The next night she was waiting for him near the gate. Her pale lamp was lit beneath a small tree about one hundred yards from the sentry post. She wore the same air of melancholy detachment he had noted in their two previous encounters. His pulse beat tumultuously as he approached her. The knowledge of her illness lent urgency to his need. That afternoon in the dispensary he had confirmed his suspicions. Tuberculosis of the lung. With a mounting sense of horror he had heard the telltale rales on both sides of her chest. His fingers had tapped out the borders of dullness in the lung tissue not expanded with air. Through the microscope he had seen the tiny flecks of red which were the bacteria of tuberculosis. He sensed that the disease process was well along and in a state of rapid advancement. He had touched her then in a different way, curiously at first, then with obvious hunger. Startled, she had arched, and turned whitened deer eyes to her shoulder, bending away like a small wild beast. Then she had seen his quivering mouth and the pain in his face and had held out her hand. Sick and exhausted, they had clung together for a moment.

He followed her now along the road, watching the small clouds of dust which rose around her feet as she stepped. The sunset smeared her skirt with scarlet, and her silver hairpin glowed like molten metal as though heated to this pitch by fires from within her. The meager traffic of the country road moved by them as on a treadmill turned to a different speed. Here and there a farmer bending beneath an A-frame piled with twigs and branches gathered from the hills for the evening cooking. A red ox led along by a rope through its nose ring, scudding at the road with frantic little bursts of side steps as it strove to keep up with the loping boy; a cart, drawn by a bicycling man, stacked with bottles of white rice wine, heading for the village.

They dreamed on, not speaking. She did not turn to see if he followed. He was ablaze with fever. Shin turned off the road and into a path between water-filled rice paddies. A length of elevated footpaths separated the pools and wound toward the smoky village below. He could see the red sky reflected in the water, dotted by the sprouts of rice. The frogs were beginning their evening cacophony, belching richly in the paddies. The rotten overripe smells of kimchi and night soil were strangely stimulating. The path coiled and uncoiled before them, turning capriciously one way, then taking an agonizing backtrack, plunging boldly forward only to swing tauntingly in a new direction. He felt that he could not bear it, that tantalizing path, that solemn promenade; that he must run, take her hand, and lead her into the darkening fields before his strength left him and he was too weak to go on.

They came to the thatched village, a cluster of mushrooms in the deepening gloom with shadowy figures squatting along the path. Heaps of small red peppers laid out to dry in the sun presented the last dim color, and a harmonica wept softly in Korean. She stopped before one of the dark mushrooms and waited for him to draw up to her, then turned into a little U-shaped courtyard. They sat on the verandalike border of the house and removed their shoes. She waited while he unlaced his heavy boots, then they passed through a sliding paper door and were alone in a darkened room.

In the absolute blackness he could hear her breathing and moved toward the sound. He reached out one hand and, comically, missed her. Now, both hands waving and swaying, hoping for contact, he turned stiffly in a halfcrouch like an automatic toy, and still he could not find her. A hand with no more substance than a moth lit upon his ear, steadying him, stopping his search. The gesture removed all awkwardness and he surrendered himself to the moth which slid now to his neck, fluttered across his lips, then flew away. She helped him with his clothing, unbuttoning his shirt, loosening his belt. There was a sudden soft impact on his shoulder as though a cat had leaped upon him. A yard of hair tumbled across his body like a waterfall. She had pulled the pin from her hair and sent it cascading. His eyes were now accommodating to the blackness and he saw her again as a cool luminescence before him. Coughing slightly, she drew him down upon the mat and laid her head upon his burning skin.

The next afternoon he had a shaking chill, and the abdominal pain returned. As dusk fell he started down the road toward the gate and then knew that he must not go. He had an abrupt premonition of his own death, that he would pour out what was left of him in a Korean hut and die here virtually unremembered, totally invisible.

The affair suddenly seemed extraterrestrial, out of humanity. There was danger in it, there was danger of being cut loose. He saw her now as the sick peasant she was; he could see her lungs, cavitary, purulent, alive with the microscopic red bacteria. He turned back toward his tent and fearfully, trembling, he lurched onto the cot, drawing the blankets about his head. He would go to the village the next night. But tonight he must sleep.

They were in a small boat on the Han River. He watched her preparing the meal, uncovering the brass bowls of cold rice and pickles, unwrapping the long-handled flat spoons. She seemed absorbed in the task, as though she were alone. She was as private as the shadow of the nostrils across her lips, a darkening in the red, subtle, unduplicable, like a signature. As hidden from him as the ecstatic air—drawn into those ovals in twin currents, to fuse, then pull lungward, diffusing through the feathery stuff of her, exchanging elements in a sublime commerce in which both were enriched, perfectly maintained. At these moments he forgot the illness that had settled there, threatening, encamped like an army.

Small waves slapped the boards of the little boat, encouraging its drift. It was an exciting sound, warm and moist like her exhalations. She told him of her uncle.

A week after her arrival at his house, the old man lay on his mat. He was coughing even then. He was turned to the wall, and each time he coughed he would draw up his knees to brace against the pain of the jostle. Sweat covered his face with countless small blisters. Now and then one of them would swell, lean toward its fellows as though making a sudden decision, and coalesce into a larger, heavier bead. In a minute (if one watched), this would begin slowly at first, then, gathering speed, roll down his face, and roll itself into extinction, leaving a shiny wet trail where it had flowed.

"I knew he would not last," said Shin. "Uncle was soon to leave. How he coughed! Each time it tore the flesh from his bones. Always he stared at the wall, absorbed by his pain. Noth-

80

ing else mattered to him, only the pain and the death that was to come."

She told of the day she knelt on the paper floor and wiped his face as she had done many times before. She had dipped a cloth into a small bowl of rice wine and squeezed a few drops into his open flaccid mouth. He did not close his lips and she heard the liquid rattling in his throat. At last she saw his neck rise and fall in the act of swallowing.

On that day Shin covered her mouth and suppressed a quiet cough herself. A little wave of weakness passed through her, and she stared at the man on the mat.

"I knew I was sick," she said. "It was the lung. I, too, had started to cough, and at night my garments were saturated with sweat, so that I would rise and change them. We were all to die with Korea."

She turned to gaze at the mountains high in the distance. The pink mist clung to them like the shimmer over hot embers.

"These are not my mountains," she said, "but I love them as I love the place of my childhood, where spring and autumn smear the countryside with colors and winter wipes it clean again for a fresh beginning."

Sloane listened as she told him how, ever since, she had been with her uncle, just the two. The others in the house were gone. Somehow the village had not been burned. She had nursed him for a year and now it was to be over.

Later she had put down the fan with which she kept the flies from his face and had gone to the house of the chief.

"My uncle is dead," she had said. "He must be buried."

The chief sighed, drew his breath in a sharp hiss, and laid his long pipe in a bowl. Then he stood and motioned her to follow. He led the way across the paddies to a hillock on the opposite side of the valley. Looking in all directions and then at the sky and again at the hill, he pointed to a spot halfway up, near a pine tree.

"He will be there," said the chief, pointing. "I will arrange it. Tomorrow he will be in the ground. Tonight I shall send my son to stand upon your rooftop and call out the Invitation to his Soul, that it may peaceably leave the house. Do not be afraid. Do you have the burial clothes?"

Shin nodded imperceptibly. For two weeks, whenever she saw her uncle had fallen into a laborious sleep she had stealthily taken the hemp material from the shelves and begun stitching together the burial clothes. At the first sign of his stirring, she would fold the material quickly and rush to the cupboard to hide it. One day as she knelt, stitching the hood, she had looked up to find his gaze fixed upon her.

Awake!

Quickly she had folded the material and covered it with her arms, but he had seen, and continued to gaze at her, not with reproach, but with a slow awakening, a little relaxation of the lines of his face, as though at that moment he suddenly understood something, had solved a mystery. They had not spoken, but a new and deeper silence came to them. There was nothing left to say, nothing of comfort or complaint, nor in fact of this world at all.

The next day the body was wrapped in the burial garments and tied around with seven ropes. Outside on the matang the men were building the coffin of poplar boards. Later they would rub it with beaten hen's egg, to give it a lacquer. In an hour the procession was on its way, in front, the coffin pulled on a ritual carriage with a flag bearing her uncle's name. Shin followed, with a handful of women mourners, whose wailing bounced off the rocky hill and echoed shrilly around her head. The coffin was lowered, foot first, head raised, and settled in that position. She turned away to look across the valley as the earth was tamped down.

From then on, Shin felt her own illness thriving, building freely in her chest, lapping at the soft inner stuff of her. It was as though, having finished with her uncle, it had turned upon her, freely now, unhampered.

She told Sloane how, in the afternoon, she would stand among the gourd vines in the tiny kitchen garden. It was such a small, closed-in, green place, where she could see things that mattered, things growing, coloring, where the slow rhythm of Korea ebbed and flowed, this year's growth aging into the soft breastlike earth, to fill it out, thickening its juice for next year's crop. The earth of her garden taught her waiting. It was a woman's teaching to a woman, and Shin listened and waited.

Sloane finished the t'akju and handed back the cup to her outstretched hand.

"I'm happy here on the river," he said. "It was good to come. Have you come here before?"

"Yes." She nodded, smiling shyly. "Many times. Last night you lay on your back with your arm across your eyes. I was silly. I wanted there to be talking, but I did not speak. So I thought, Tomorrow we will go together to the river Han with its ten thousand flashings. There will be a small boat and we will go into it. I will paddle for a while to a place where the lotus floats, and under their dark leaves the darker fish lie breeding. We will have food in a wicker box and t'akju for you to drink and grow merry. I have never seen you merry! Then we will drift, winding up the silver ribbon of the stream. Yes, I will wind up the river in a silver ball and give it to you. I will lie in your arms and we will see together the mist along the cliffs where the white heron nests."

That night, Sloane had left the village rather late. It was particularly dark, there being no moon. He switched a flashlight on and off to help negotiate a turn and get himself oriented in the right direction. It was exhilarating to walk in the dark with the sensation of not being quite sure of one's footing or of one's bearings. It was a groping, aided now and then by an intuitive spark. What made it so delicious a game was the element of uncertainty and the low stakes. One could always wait for the dawn.

He reached the edge of the village and flashed his light along the mound of earth that walled in the rice fields, looking for the path. Smugly he noted it to be but a few feet from his present position and, climbing the slight embankment, he switched off the light and floated along the path, a disembodied concentrate of blackness undistinguished from the night. It was absolutely calm; no intrusion of wind, noise, or smell. He might have been blind. It was a luxurious perversion of the senses. To experience thus the loss or absence of vision, to quicken his hearing, smell, and touch as he had read the blind do, to listen for the friction of a shoot of rice upon its fellow, to hear the young of the cuckoo flopping in their nest, to become aware of a fog by the richness of the air upon his face. And how infinitely more delectable the comfort of being able to salvage all, to recoup the losses by the flick of a flashlight switch.

He had progressed halfway across the valley, sure now of his direction. He could see the lights of the valley suspended in the blackness. It was difficult to convince himself that the cluster of twinkling lights in the void midway between earth and sky was his destination. The edges of reality were blurred. Which would endure and which was the dream, the black valley of Korea or the military post in the sky? There was a kind of magic to that military post, however. At a given signal it could whisk off carpetlike and carry him back to Connecticut. This other world, the blind, calm Korean night, this one wasn't quite so safe. There was no way back. There was only the groping black present. And perhaps, perhaps he would lose the flashlight, or the batteries might run out. But was he alive now, or would he be when he reached those lights?

That first sound reached his awareness long after he had heard the small thudding noise. It came from somewhere in the rice paddy on his left. A second later he heard the tiny splash of a frog jumping from the water. That was from his right. He was listening now, awake and quickened: a low grunting and the slight sizzle that a cigarette makes when it is arced into the water from behind. Then he was walking rapidly, the pulse hammering in his neck. Fear had sprung, a full-grown phantom exactly his size, and had clicked into place in his body. Blind and not daring to use the light, his nostrils raised in the air fighting to control the sound of the breaths that were so hard to take in, and once having been drawn were not enough to sustain the heightened heart and brain. At the sound of the running feet directly ahead of him he was a fainting wild-eyed beast.

He flicked on the flashlight. Five wisp-whiskered faces, their cheekbones and brows heightened by his low-held light, were closed upon him, blocking escape on all sides. They would kill me for my boots alone, he thought. To die here in this mud, blind and wasted—not wasted, he thought bitterly; the rice would be especially green here next year. Could he speak, could he save enough air from each gasp to put together a few words, to beg for his life? Would they wait long enough, would they know? What were the words in Korean? What were they? He could see now the glint of metal in the beam of light.

"Nanung ouisa imnidda. I am a doctor, you must not hurt me. My friends in the village will kill you. Tomorrow they will come to see me and they will know."

From somewhere he had drawn the words, snorted them out hysterically, and waited. They, too, had paused and were waiting. He pointed to his boots. He sat down on the ground and took them off. Next he slipped out of his jacket and trousers. He piled the cap and the remainder of his clothing on the ground and waited. They had not moved. Blind and naked, he waited. They waited also.

There was a sudden jolting pain in his temple. He had not seen his assailant raise the rock, but he knew at the moment of its contact with his crunching, splitting flesh that they would not kill him. The Koreans did not kill like that. Full of hope, he surrendered to the outpouring of his consciousness and fell from the path into the rancid mud.

Days later, he had spent the night in Shin's hut. There was a solemnity about the way she undressed him, loosening his belt, removing his shirt, folding it with infinite care, smoothing it over and over with her hands. At one point she raised the folded khaki shirt to her face and pressed it over her, inhaling, taking no notice of him then, drawing into herself the smell of it, enjoying his vapor, as though in the absence of his flesh his spirit would do as well.

At first he had been impatient to the point of annoyance. These slow rituals made him hard, brutal. When at last she crept to his side, his force made her gasp, but she made no sound, keeping the envelope of sadness about her. It was this sorrowing kind of lovemaking that now excited him beyond anything he had known. Certainly it was not like Kate's, all jollity and health; Kate, who made love with the clear blind understanding that she would live forever, that death was never, that she and Sloane were somehow gloriously chosen for perfect endless copulation.

Shin seemed always to be using her last breaths. His lengthy kisses all but sucked the heart from her throat. And she welcomed the pain and sweetness even as she understood well that it was her doom she embraced. Each time their passion broke, it was as though she took one step closer to it. Still she drew him back and in, dying as eagerly, as closely as possible, wanting it to last forever, never to end.

"Why are you always so sad?" he asked her.

"Not sad." She smiled. "Not sad. Too happy."

His own lovemaking had changed, taken on the wisdom and restraint that she seemed to have been born with. Her slim body to him, his ear pressed to her neck, listening to her blood, supporting her upon him, turning her with a delicacy that surprised him, as though they were moving together in a fragile web that any roughness would destroy. He had never been tender until Shin.

"What time is it?"

The weariness flattened his voice, muffled it so that it was indistinct even to his own ears. Even as he asked, the question seemed superfluous. When no answer came, he stepped from the door of the dispensary and stared down at the road. He knew she was there waiting for him around the bend, wiping her cheeks now and again with a piece of folded cloth. It was a little worrying gesture, like wringing one's hands or a deep, breath-catching sigh. For the past two hours, as the line of patients shortened, he had fought against the thought of her. He had gone through the mechanics of sick call, listening to the telling of symptoms, the examinations, the treatments, and all the while in his mind the white speck that was Shin was growing larger and larger, taking up more of his consciousness. With the departing bow of the last patient, his whole brain would be filled with her, not another bit of room. It was a usurpation; implacable, it was true, but longed for and gentle and always perfectly timed, as though she held back her nearness until the patients had all been seen, waiting her turn, knowing that he would come.

"I'm leaving!" he called back over his shoulder. There was a pause and he waited for the answer.

"Yes, Sir Doc," came the drawling reply.

He started down the road but stopped at a burst of loud laughter from the dispensary. In sudden fury he turned to retrace his steps, then stopped as the men's voices became audible.

"Doc's dippin' his wick tonight."

"No, sir!" That was Jang. Sloane could picture him shaking his head so hard his cheeks flapped.

"Aw, cut it out, Jang. You know fuckin' well Doc's goin' to the village to see his moose. Meets her down the road every night."

"No, sir!" came Jang's voice, harder now, almost angry.

"What the hell do you care if he does? Even Doc's got to have a little push-push now and then."

Sloane could imagine the lewd descriptive gesture that he used, pushing his index finger in and out of a circle made by the opposite thumb and forefinger. This was a boy named Johnson, a clerk. He'd find a way of getting even secretly, the stupid bastard.

"Shut up!" barked Jang, and Sloane heard the defiant slow stamp of boots across the floor. Jang was going to fight for him, defend his honor. He had done it before—slammed his fist into a mouth that was too freely opened where Sloane was concerned.

Sloane thought he'd better go in and stop it, but then did not act. Let Jang hit him; serve him right. Jang was by far the strongest one in the company. Slow to anger, and then only on Sloane's account, but with those murderous fists. He had watched Jang settle an account with another Korean soldier. Jang had called to him, a staccato barking sound that the other recognized as a threat or insult, stepping up to accept the challenge. It had been a very workmanlike display of strength and fury. The other man never landed a blow. Sloane had let Jang hit him three times and then yelled from his window:

"Stop that! No fighting around here, you understand?" But his heart wasn't in it. In fact he felt pleasure in the comfort of Jang's strength and friendship. How many people had someone who would die for them?

But the talking stopped abruptly and he knew he had been seen and a secret signal given by the men to each other. He stepped inside and grinned at the Korean, still clenching his fists. Pointedly, he said to Johnson:

"I'll be with my friend in the village if you need me. And, Johnson . . ."

"Yes, sir. Yes, sir."

"I should like just once to leave this dispensary without listening to you shoot your dirty brains off."

"Yes, sir!" The "sir" vibrated like a metal rod.

Sloane turned, hating himself for having said it. Halfway down the hill, he again heard laughter, but by now he was indifferent to it, heading down into the valley to Shin.

She was standing beneath an old knobby pine tree, all of whose branches reached away from the road toward the rice fields beyond, as though entreating the other green things not to abandon it there by the road.

Shin stood behind the tree, her back also to the road, leaning against it. Sloane quickened his pace and when he was close enough to touch her, spoke softly so as not to startle her.

"Shin."

She turned unsmiling, but with a serenity to her expression that was almost fervent. They walked together, sensing each other's relief. A wheel had turned again and by some miraculous chance they had come together once more. Each time they met it was like that—a stroke of great good luck, a miracle that might never happen again.

Usually it was after dark when he entered the village, and although everyone knew he was there in the hut, the fact of not having been actually seen was somehow insulating. This time, the sun had not set, and they walked silently along, their faces downcast. Out of the corner of his eye Sloane saw the familiar faces of his patients watching them, some concealing smiles behind their hands, others stony-faced, severe. Sloane knew she was suffering on his account, paying the whole price, in fact, while he was getting off scot-free. The Koreans hated her because of him, would happily have stoned her, and might still were it not for his presence on the hill and their absolute need of him. Somehow he knew that to them, what the whores were doing was not as bad as her offense, which was repugnant to them precisely because she was not a whore but one of them, a working peasant, and so all the more a traitor to her people. She bore their scorn in silence, outwardly ignoring the muttered curses, the undisguised contempt. His cheeks burned for her. He wanted to take her hand, put his arm around her waist and lead her along, but he did not dare, or rather, had not the courage to.

There was a commotion in the matang of one of the huts, a three-sided one with stone walls, the home of a wealthy farmer. A small group of people were huddled around a construction of some kind. Two of them were beating it with heavy sticks. He stopped directly in front of the matang. With mounting horror he saw that two poles had been sunk into the ground about three feet apart. Between these two poles there had been strung a dog, its tail and hind legs tied to one, its head and forepaws to the other. The animal hung thus between the poles. It was alive, its mouth hanging weakly open, drops of saliva falling from the tongue. Occasionally it would whimper and thrust its body upward in an effort to break free. The effort quickly exhausted it and the animal would slump limply again. The belly of the beast was swollen to monstrous proportions so that it resembled a hugely pregnant bitch, although Sloane could see that it was a male. The skin over the belly was stretched tight and the pink hairs bristled. As Sloane watched, two men began to beat the dog with sticks, forcefully but obviously not using full strength. The blows were rained on the back, flanks, belly, and legs. The head was carefully avoided.

Sloane called to Shin, who had stopped a few feet away from him and, face downcast, was waiting for him to move on.

"Shin, what are they doing?"

With what seemed a great effort, she turned to gaze at the

scene for a long moment, then looked away. There was no surprise in her actions, no horror, no revulsion, none of the outrage and disgust that he felt welling up in him.

"It's cruel! Why are they doing that?"

In a very low voice she explained, shaking her head. "Not cruel. People make food."

"Are they going to eat that dog?" He was incredulous. "Well, all right; if they are, why don't they just kill it and be done with it? Why are they torturing it to death?"

"Not cruel," she repeated. "The people give the dog much rice, too much rice, every day for two months. Make very fat. All day push rice into dog's mouth, make fat, good taste. Now beat him to make soft, tender, good to eat. Pretty soon dog die, then cook in fire. Very good food for my people."

My God, thought Sloane, his stomach contracting in nausea, how can they do it? The rhythmic thumping of the sticks on the dog's flesh, first one, then the other, was maddening to him. He had an impulse to run and grab their arms, order them to stop, then cut down the beast.

Shin must have sensed his thoughts. Stepping to him, she touched his sleeve.

"Come now," she said quickly. "It is good. You do not know this."

He allowed himself to be led away, gazing back at the scene as though unable to accept its reality.

He unlaced his boots and pulled them off, leaving them outside on the matang. The floor of the Korean house welcomed his feet with the warmth from the earthen flues that ran beneath it. These herded the hot smoke from the kitchen cooking stove under the entire house, before discharging it in a fanning cloud at the opposite end. He had always marveled at the simplicity and ingenuity of this heating system. The heat was steady and even and made sleeping on the floor a pure pleasure. He never slept so well as in this house.

That night they did not make love. Sloane felt feverish and still nauseated. When Shin had undressed him and seen that his body did not respond to her, she had covered him with a quilt and watched him fall asleep. When he awoke, it was to utter blackness. For a moment he did not know where he was and started up. Her hand on his cheek stopped him and he sank back to the floor mat. She lit a kerosene lamp, and in its shuddering light he saw again the dog swaying between the poles. He struggled achingly to his feet.

"I must go," he whispered. "It is late."

She helped him dress with great tenderness as though they had just made love, the warmth still within her. At the door he turned and took her fiercely, almost crushingly, in his arms for a brief moment, then slid open the door and slipped out into the courtyard. He did not look back until he reached the road. When he did, he saw the slender pillar of wavering light where the door had not been closed all the way.

Sloane stepped into the little kitchen garden. Within the confines of the tall bamboo fence the moonlight seemed concentrated, bleaching to pallor the grotesque gourds. It was as though they had melted in the sun and run limply into these fierce elongated shapes, then, hardened again by the cold moon, had been fixed forever, the lame and twisted hunchbacks of the garden.

He lit a cigarette and in the breathless air the smoke clung and clustered like ectoplasm. She knows, he thought. There was something on her face; it was more than an expression—more like the spoor of an animal. He had gazed at it while she slept, searching, tracking the beast that eluded him there. It scampered from her mouth to her eyes, hiding beneath the lids, only to emerge and dart fleetingly across to her ears, becoming lost in the black forest above. It was a knowledge that she had, and that he sought.

He heard a soft sound, like the falling of a leaf, and knew it was her footstep even before he turned to see her. There was a silence about them that was difficult to break, as though the air itself had hardened into glass which encased them, making the transmission of sounds, even the movement of lips, impossible. She came and leaned against his arm. She seemed weightless, as though much of her had lightened into dust and blown away. He himself was weighted, leaden. He felt the need to break the silence, to speak, but the effort to think was too great. He could not find anything to say. In the end he placed his hand upon the back of her neck, cupping it. His resting fingers felt the trill of her pulse, rapid and shallow, a fainting pulse, the pulse of a little animal he had trapped. He had it beneath his fingertips and knew then, and without words, what she knew —that it was over, that he would not come to her again.

As he turned to leave, she remained standing, her back to him as though hiding something. He remembered a story she had told him about a princess whose lover had left her. In the end the girl had turned into rain so that she could beat down upon him, flood him, "but warmly, warmly, that he might remember."

The night was graying as he walked from the village, and the lark's tongue vibrated in his ear.

A velvet evening had settled imperceptibly over Korea. Wisps of lavender smoke hung here and there above thatched roofs. There was no breeze to stir it. Above all, there was no sound, as though it were a painting—russet, sere, green, fading. What gave the painting life was the transmitted quivering of the rice, germinating, growing, waving in terraced fields everywhere. He could feel the life in the sodden ground bursting up, wildly exuberant, fed by the wet dust of layers of ancestors who had eaten rice here and entered the paddies at last to give life to the next generation.

He rose and entered the dispensary.

"Anyone else?" Sloane stared at his hands. The fading sun made a viny pattern behind them on the tabletop. All day he had experienced subterranean quakes in his body. Fatigue, which came like the shifting of rocks and earth in his center; which, when it had passed, when the matter settled into its new place, left him lessened somehow in spirit and substance as well, he was certain. He had decided that the inability of matter to be destroyed was in the most limited, puristic sense only. Of course it could be destroyed. The holes, the empty spaces inside of him were proof.

"I go see, Sir Doc," came the answer. "Yes, Sir Doc, nobody inside, onry outside. Mama-san, baby come more s'coshi. Pretty soon here."

Sloane sat at the table, idly making shadow pictures in the small orange beam, until with sudden rudeness it was gone, taking with it the illusion of warmth as well. He felt unreasonably colder and hurt. He had a revulsion for the act of childbirth that had survived his medical school training not lessened now by the announcement of another obstetrical case—a difficult one, he knew, since the normal ones never came to him but took place on the warm floors and under the drifting chimney smoke of the Korean houses. Only a little mound of blood and tissue on the rice straw, cleaned up by the kind of quiet competence seen in old arthritic hands. The complicated ones, bled out, battered, cramped to an ominous inertia in which both host and parasite lay dissipated, staring ahead at the newly realized possibility of disaster, these were the ones he saw. They took a daring, a bravado, an egotism that he no longer felt. With great effort he pushed the chair back and stood up and walked to the open door of the dispensary just as the sun sizzled out.

Sloane saw the two figures leaving a cluster of huts and inching single file along the narrow raised embankments which served as footpaths between the rice paddies. As they drew nearer Sloane could see the long skirts billowing about them, a sliver of the setting sun caught in their silver hairpins, their faces expressionless, like docile beasts who register neither joy nor pain. The older woman bent upon her stick, the younger round, pausing to rest, one hand pressing the unborn child beneath her waistband.

Suddenly he knew it was Shin. Look at her, thought Sloane, as he stood outside the dispensary watching her slow climb. She is Korea. Thin, short of breath, using up her last strength to roll that great inappropriate belly up the hill. Korea raped. I did it, we're doing it, we're screwing this country.

Nevertheless he did not go down the path to meet her. He waited at the top, feeling the twilight fall softly against him in suffocating purple waves. Her head was bowed, and with each step she lifted her abdomen with her hands as though to roll it forward, a hiss coming through her stiffly parted lips. Ten feet away from him and still at a lower level, she stopped and raised her head only so far as to include his booted feet in her field of vision.

For a long time she stood holding herself rigidly bent, as though waiting for him to speak or walk to her. Then she made a profound bow which caused her to wobble dangerously as her center of gravity shifted. At that, he stepped quickly forward and raised her. Her face was impervious, unreadable.

The two women followed Sloane to the treatment room, closed off partially from the rest of the Quonset hut by white plywood partitions. A homemade wooden table covered with Korean newspapers occupied the center of the room. A small table of bottles, packages, and trays stood against one wall. A tall operating-room lamp and a stool completed the furnishings. He gave the old woman a pile of newspapers and signaled her to help Shin undress, lie on the table, and cover herself with the paper. While waiting, Sloane walked outside and lit a cigarette. When the paper stopped rustling, he reentered the room. Shin's eyes were barely open, as though to filter the scene of all but the barest essentials. In her hands she held a smooth stick of hard wood. She would grasp it tightly with each contraction, the only outward sign of her distress. There was an embarrassed silence between them. Sloane motioned the old woman to leave.

"Where have you been?" he asked her, hating himself for making the question sound like a demand. Surely he had no rights where she was concerned.

"The house of my uncle," she replied.

"I heard nothing . . ." he began, but she had raised one palm up, arching her wrist backward, silencing him.

Later Jang told him of her ostracism by the villagers, their contempt for her as the whore of an American officer. In the beginning they had thrown stones at the house and knocked down the kimchi jars in the matang and punched holes in the bamboo fence. But when her pregnancy became obvious, they let her alone, only spitting and cursing as they passed the house and saw her kneeling before the grinding stone.

Sloane imagined her never looking up, bearing their cruelty in silence, even indifference. As her time drew near, an old mama-san of the village had come to live with her, to help with the food and chores. It was she who had come with Shin to the dispensary.

She lay on the delivery table shuddering with her contractions. There was something about her which reminded him of the dog he had seen, hanging and beaten, its great swollen body stuffed with rice. It was the air of the victim. He recoiled from the thought in guilt.

The contractions were three minutes apart. Jang had told him that Shin had been in labor for twenty-four hours. She appeared weary and wan. Sloane gave her a sedative and sat down on a stool to wait. As the hours went by, he noticed a dismaying lack of progress. There was no descent, no dilatation, no change save for a barely perceptible intermittent slowing of the fetal heart. He spoke slowly and carefully to her from time to time. "Do not worry." "You will be all right." "God be with you." She smiled faintly, whispering her thanks with the slightest exhalation.

Morning had come barely noticed. He felt uplifted and frightened by her struggle. Burning white knuckles strained to break through the skin. A quiet hiss came through clenched teeth in soft bursts. A swatch of black hair escaped upon the table, and through its filigree one could see the characters of the Korean newspaper spread beneath her body. Sloane stared at the newsprint as if it were a coded message from some ancient Oriental midwife who had fathomed the secrets of childbirth in this land, and who had plied her trade through quiet centuries in a manner leathery, silent, and brave. If he could but read from those characters her fearless instructions, he would have it then, the way to save these two—not even that; the way to endure it with them.

Sloane sat by her cot. His fingers slipped from the pulse at her wrist to the hollow of her palm, and he clasped it tightly until the contraction was over. Like a husband. He spoke:

"Shin?"

She turned her head slowly toward him. He pointed to her abdomen, touching it with his finger, then transferred the finger to his own chest.

"Is it mine?"

She stared at him for a long time, then nodded slightly.

Somehow the change in the position of their hands had seemed to unlock them from a constriction. She was talking now, rather singing out words, softly and continuously. When the pain was at its height her voice became indefinite, slurred, and he was unable to understand any of her words. Once when she fell silent he asked:

"Is the pain too bad?"

"I do not care."

"I am sorry," whispered Sloane, his eyes closing in tear-blindness.

Shin's voice resumed in breathless monologue:

"The plum blossom arrives while there is still snow on the ground. It is a surprise. The flower of first love. In the spring garden the high rocks are covered with moss. The stone water basins look young despite their great age. We used to catch dragonflies there. Such fun! Grandfather came home to be ready for death. Remember? He was very old, very beautiful, with his calm round face, gray hair, and long beard. All his life he took everything as it came. How beautiful his death was, quiet and peaceful, without wrestling. His married daughters had all come home to be with him. As soon as breath had passed, my uncle took a shirt of Grandfather's and went up on top of the grass roof. He shook it three times and waved farewell to the spirit.

" 'Chuksam kache kasiow.' Oh, take with you this shirt.

"Then the wailing began, low and rhythmical, mounting.

" 'Ai-kyo. Ai-kyo. Uyi. Uyi.' Sorrow. Sorrow.

"They placed him in a coffin of thick strong pine, in which only pine nails were used. Pine shows the stillness of the dead, and also protects him from insects. High, high in the mountains he was carried by his neighbors and family to the place of his grave. Nearby was a temple of red stone with roofs like tiled boats, for the ends turned up like keels. On the way back we heard the tongueless bells struck by the swinging log. How sweet the air was, hushed and ghost-colored."

For an entire day Shin had lain there, with sweat and flies

upon her face, ignoring them both. For hours Sloane had sat, straining in wordless dialogue with that bursting womb. For hours he had known that it would end badly, that in another few hours he would see the hands relax around the clutched stick, see it fall gracelessly to the ground, see the flies crawl, dauntless now, into the nostrils beneath the rounded moons of her cheeks.

Suddenly he knew that normal childbirth was impossible. There were useless, feeble contractions of an exhausted womb battering against an unyielding cervix. It would be necessary to cut the cervix widely and withdraw the baby with obstetrical forceps—a pair of cupped blades to be applied separately, then hinged together at the handle. But where in rural Korea could one find obstetrical forceps, a refinement of civilized medicine? In any case, the maneuver would be exceedingly hazardous; the hemorrhage could very likely prove exsanguinating.

Not an obstetrician, Sloane had never performed such an operation, had only recollections of medical school texts to guide him. His fear gave urgent authority to his voice as he called:

"Jang!"

The Korean clomped across the floor in heavy boots.

"Yes, Sir Doc."

"Where is the nearest provincial hospital?"

"Kaesong, I think, Sir Doc."

"How far?"

"Almost eight hours, Sir Doc."

She would never survive the trip over those deeply rutted roads. He scratched the words "obstetrical forceps" on a piece of paper, signed his name, and gave it to Jang.

"Go now. Take the jeep and driver—fast. When you get there, find someone who speaks English. Give him this and bring back the package."

Jang nodded, flooding his features with a smile. Sloane had

learned not to return those smiles. It usually turned out to be inappropriate. In fact he had never been able to interpret the Korean smile, often mirthless, edged with embarrassment, like a reflex act touched off by any sort of stimulus, be it pleasurable or noxious. Jang was gone. It was not without a touch of envy that Sloane watched him leave, ordered from the unanesthetized core of the experience, given a specific function—orders to be carried out.

Sloane ached for the sound of a public address system in a hospital, to which he could run and call out the words that would bring immediate help:

"Inhalation therapy—intensive care unit—stat—inhalation therapy—intensive care unit—stat." The voice on the public address system is nasal, uninflected, the words hurtling out like those of a tobacco auctioneer. "Stat" means right away, now or never, emergency. It isn't how she says it, it is what she says that makes you pause wherever you are in that hospital, makes an exactly you-sized shadow of fear click into place in your body. In the cafeteria the secretaries' forks pause, too, cole slaw at lip, while strands fall back into the plate. They are like deer which stop in their grazing at the distant roll of thunder, grass protruding from their mouths. Slow, grave-faced painters pause over their pails, dipping brushes, wiping them more carefully than ever, as though the emergency page is a spell that has been cast, a magical utterance which instantly enchants. They are no longer, nor ever again will be exactly what they had been before. There is a common look on faces as though each were alone in a mansion and suddenly heard a tune played on a music box somewhere. The kind of thing that made old Catholics cross themselves, and old Jews spit over their shoulder.

Just to know that on these very premises lies a blue-faced gasper, a flailer, eyes bulging with the precognition of death. Skin cold, clammy, disgusting to the touch. (I don't like the feel of death sweat, Sloane thought; it is so cold and thick.) See how

100

he strains to take in one more breath, thrusting, stretching forward his head, dilating his nostrils, heaving the sticky bellows in his rigid barrely chest just one more time, then gathering for the next, without respite. How hungry are the heart and brain when lung can find no air for them! Cell after cell swells up and bursts with a kind of silent implosion, until enough are dead so that the rest, pulled into captivity, follow suit with resignation automatically, blackening.

I have been there before, he thought, one of the white-coated tenders, bending over the struggle and rage. Awkward storks, rocketing our heads up and down, turning to each other jerkily for corroboration, or in dismay or indifference. Doing things (Doctors, do something!) while in the cellophane tent the dead-elect lolls, empurpled as autumn, soon all thumped out, fresh meat, packaged in plastic. But first the ceremony. Needles are sunk in the flesh of the arms and legs, the heart, even. The body is draped with cords and tubes, festooned as any bride. Beep-beep-beep, intones the monitor in a prayer for the dying. Beep-beep . . . beep-beep-beep . . . in a kittenish, little girly voice. . . .

A sudden jerk of his head informed Sloane that he had been dozing.

Midday held its breath, unwilling to relieve the humid pressure with a single exhalation. A day had passed. A day of whispers, rustles, and panic. The heartbeat slowed, was barely perceptible beneath the protuberance of the abdomen. The newspaper was marked with red in an ever-increasing stain. Her eyes roved slowly in the blindness of exhaustion and pain. Occasionally they met his, fastened for an instant, and moved on. Outside, the old woman waited, crouched down, quiet, exuding silent despair. Shin seemed to him an earth-filled bottle into which had been dropped a seed. The grown plant had filled the bottle, with roots and convolutions, and needed release from its glass prison, in order to live in the air and rain. It could not be drawn through the narrow neck without sundering it from the roots. He could rip it from the bottle's neck and watch it wilt untethered from life. He could smash the bottle into fragments with a hammer, pick up the freed green, and place it in the largeness of the earth. Or he could wait, holding the glass, watching the light glisten on its smoothness, and wait.

Then suddenly the waiting was over. Jang had returned, a dusty, sweaty angel carrying a shapeless parcel. Sloane unwrapped it swiftly and held it to the light. In his hand was a single shining metal instrument—one blade of a pair of obstetrical forceps, one useless blade—"Made in Germany" on the handle—one blade. The difference between an instrument and a weapon was one more blade of an obstetrical forceps. Sloane had an impulse to laugh, and as swiftly it was gone. Holding the blade like a club, he was tempted to smash out against Jang, who smiled now in expected approbation, or to fling it across the room. In the end, he laid it carefully like a piece of fragile glass that might be scratched by the slightest trauma, and turned slowly toward the table.

Once again, he sat at Shin's feet, and cut deeply into the womb neck. Her warm blood cascaded over his hands and hung in rivulets from his elbows, then ran into his armpits and down his sides. Reaching into the torrent, Sloane felt a foot, and then he pulled, knees, thighs, buttocks, cord, shoulders, and arms, then head, then blood. A gurgling sound, a cry, a life, and a death. He placed the crying infant on the dead girl's breast and watched the stick slip from her pale hand to the floor with the faintest of clatters.

Little Saint Hugh

Saint Hugh's Tale

In a doorway Belaset stood, her dark skin flaming in the sunset. For a long time she gazed as though to enthrall me. Then urgent, she held out her arm, offering me an apple, bidding me take it. I ran to her, glancing back to see if anyone were witness. It was her *heart* cupped there in the palm of her hand. For a long time I stood holding it until the sun fell to the knife of the horizon. Belaset paled, whitened so suddenly it seemed the vanishing sun had made her so, or that terrible gift of her heart. At last it was just an apple in my hand that was red. I turned and ran, looking back once to see her fluttering like a prayer shawl in the doorway. And then I fell, and only let the apple drop from my fingers when I died.

Beatrice will come in her grief. For twenty-six days I lay beneath the filth waiting for my mother. I was quiet and patient as I could be. She must come in time, I knew. I had only to wait, and try very hard to be good. Still, twenty-six days . . . such a long time with ears and eyes stopped, my mouth full of mud. Beatrice did not come. It was Copin who found me when, swollen with gases, I floated to the top and burst. Of course by then my body had started to sing, and I was feeling the first faint intimations of immortality.

How deep the well of the Jew. Moss grows there upon the stones and near the bottom. I was the first to see it, to brush it with my cheek as I fell, oh, slowly fell, tumbling into the shaft. The moss comforted me, to see a thing that lived unnoticed in the Jew's well forever. Already my body had begun to sing, a great sound I did not make with my throat. It was like a vapor coming off me, as though I steamed into singing, and grew substanceless in the doing, less and less flesh, more and more sound, pure and rare and high. I was eight years old or twelve or somewhere between. It does not matter, for now I am Enshrined, Engulfed in Eternity, in the cathedral of Lincoln. Bishops pray before my crypt and call me Little Saint Hugh.

I do not know why I was beckoned to the Jewish Quarter. Someone's heart seemed to require me. Beatrice, my mother, had said, "Go not near the Jews at Passover, for they do murder such blond little men as you, and draw off blood to mix with dough for their unleavened bread." Yet Passover is in the spring, and it was August when I died. There was a great wedding among them. Belaset was to be married. Dark Belaset, gold Belaset. Belaset, deepest blackest river flowing from the Jews into the sea. I had loved her always, and now she was to be married. The town was bearded with Jews from every corner of England, come down for the feast. Was it she furtive and afraid, who summoned me, skulking at their edge? I would not have wished to destroy them, those many Jews, my Belaset, but I floated to the surface and they found me, Copin found me, and called the others. Their caftans stank from cess as they lifted me from the muck whispering terror out of their beards. What to do? I must be hid. They would be accused! The gentiles would kill them! Where should they hide me? So small, I could fit in the well shaft in Copin's house, and there I was carried, my hair matted with offal. They turned me into the well, where I dropped like the first bloody leaf of September, slowly rocking down into the cold black water.

But I had already started to sing, celestial notes rising from the depth of the shaft, reverberant. How they trembled when they heard me, and knew I would be discovered. Poor Jews. They did not kill me. I fell and drowned. But it does not matter now, for I have risen beyond all that. Fact or fancy, it is of little moment now. I was chosen, and the path to sainthood led through Jewish blood. I would have rather grown up, and lived. What is sainthood but an overleaping of life? What laughter is there for a boy in martyrdom? There is only the steady cool thrill of eternity.

Copin's Tale

One ill begets two, which breed four, and so on, until the earth is swarming with irretrievable misdeeds. How could I know when I heard that music and followed its siren to the privy that it drew me to my last losing? There, floating on his side, lay the little boy, his pale arms strewn as in sleep about his yellow hair, lipping the swill unconcerned. I was frightened, and ran to fetch the others, Mordecai and Issachar, and the rest. "Here now, Copin," they scolded. "Herd your thoughts lest evil stray like a wolf into your ear and pounce upon your brain." Thus they chided until they too stood in the stenchy evening air, and saw those folded limbs, that ghastly head. Then they, too, were stricken. I heard their gasps, and knew that we were lost, bereft of hope. We could but enact our terror, skim the body from the pool, and carry him to my house to lie at the bottom of my well. After the wedding we would take him up and bury him elsewhere. So it was concurred.

But an odor stole from my well, a honeyed odor such as I have never known. It settled on my clothing, filling the house with its mist, then poured from the windows. I raced to shut them, pulled the shutters, bolted the door. Still it rose and floated. My house contained a cloud of great sweetness. I inhaled it and felt it in my chest coiling and uncoiling. The others came and breathed it in wonder and fear. The odor would reveal us. We must caulk the floors and ceiling, the walls. Brick in the fireplace, lest it billow forth over Lincoln, spelling out in wisps the place where the boy lay. The woman Beatrice smelt it in her bed, and rose. She came to stand outside my house, and peered at the rosy smoke that spilled from the rafters, and knew her son was there, in my house, and she screamed.

Bailiffs came, one on either side of the fainting woman, and behind them wriggled the mob, pointing its chins in the air to sniff the pale issue of my chimney. With each step nearer to my house the faces grew deeper and deeper red, until in the torchlight I could see a thousand furious feet stamp on those cobblestones, pressing through the narrows of the Bailgate, hurtling down Steep Hill toward the bottom, and me.

Terrible sights. Beatrice untwisting from the arms of the men to point her rigid finger, the red glow of the mob, saliva and sweat. Suddenly there mounted in me a feeling of guilt at least as passionate as their hatred. I wanted to be not me, but one of them, to share with them an action against some common enemy, to ask for the death of the Jews, of whom I, Copin, was one. Good people, I did no killing. There was no murder by the Jews. Then why this guilt? Can so many be wrong? People of Lincoln, we did not do this thing. Stop, stop. One moment for the truth. There was a boy who fell into the cesspool and drowned. I found his body, and put it here in my well. It was foolish, I know, but you must understand we were frightened. It has the appearance of murder, but the appearance only.

Yet there was a man of elegant mien who separated from the van of the throng and alone entered my house. John de Lexinton. Sir, sir, I implore you, keep them from me. I am innocent. He wooed me with his beautiful eyes, blue and honest, that by their gaze held back my killers. Straight into my heart he

106

peered, upon his mouth a tiny wanton curve of encouragement. I loved John de Lexinton. Everything about him was noble, his robe and cap, his stance, And upon his index finger rode the King's seal. He spoke as from a great height.

"We have heard sometimes that Jews have dared to attempt such things in insult of our crucified Lord, Jesus Christ."

Then in a low conspiratorial tone:

"Wretched man, dost thee not know that a speedy end awaits thee? All the gold in England would not ransom thee. Yet, unworthy though thou art, I will tell thee how thou canst save life and limb from destruction. Both of these will I save thee if, without fear or falsehood, thou wilt expose unto me all that has been done in this matter."

Even before he had spoken I was seduced. What charm, what power. Now he offered me life. Adoring, I answered.

"My lord John, I will show wondrous things unto thee."

Again and again his eyelight urged me.

"What the Christians say is true. Every year the Jews crucify a boy in injury and insult to Jesus. This they do privately, in remote and secret places. This boy whom they call Hugh, our Jews stole and crucified without mercy, and after he was dead and they wished to hide his corpse, they could not bury nor conceal it. In the morning when they thought it was hidden away, the earth vomited and cast it forth. There it lay unburied on the ground, to the horror of the Jews. At length they threw it into my well, but still they could not hide it, for the mother never wearied in her search, and found him."

When I had finished, a great silence filled the house, as much from the consternation of the people who had heard my confession as from the sudden discontinuance of the music which had come from the well. It was as though what was needed for the boy to rest in peace was in fact my falsest statement. And with the singing departed the censing angels and that odor of orchard and Heaven. The quiet was broken by an old blind

107

woman, who knelt before the boy and wept, "O my poor little Hugh, to have died this way." Then she wiped her shriveled sockets with moisture from the boy's body, and rose to her feet unblinded, seeing.

Seated in their midst I wrote:

Know ye. The boy, Hugh, son of Beatrice, was enticed by Belaset, daughter of Benedick, with an apple in her outstretched hand. He came within and was seized by the Jews, who crucified him for ten days in mimicry of Jesus Christ. When, at last, he died, his blood was drawn and smeared upon our bread in the tradition of the Israelites. Many Jews were summoned from far and wide for the rites. They are all knowledgeable and blameworthy. The boy was buried then but the earth cast him forth. Therefore we threw him into the well. I, Copin, swear this to be a true and faultless remark upon the death of Little Hugh.

"Seize him!" cried John de Lexinton, as I signed the paper. I was not altogether shocked. He had, after all, to make some show of his resolve prior to my release. The others had all been taken. From my doorway I watched. How quietly they went, Aaron, Moshe, tethered Abraham, and Belaset, all, submitting silent as oxen. They were dressed as though for winter despite the summer heat, the women in kerchiefs, the men hatted and wrapped, each carrying his little velvet bag of phylacteries. Later, in the Tower, they would face the eastern wall, and the sound of their droning would soothe the women until, still feverish from prayer, they would turn at last from the stones and smile at each other, risen.

I alone was freed. And will not before any man say that I did not enjoy my freedom, my life, even as my brethren languished and died. That perjury I shall not commit. For even then, especially then, I loved the act of living, and the promise of it, above all else, above God. I lived and was free.

Yet the King read that which I had signed. And flew, I am told, into a rage of terrible proportion, demanding that I be taken and hanged. King Henry desires me hanged. For a Jew to be hanged is for him to be high. At the order of a king, it is higher still. I believed in John de Lexinton. I believed that he would save me. I mistook him. Which brings me to my hanging.

Neck-knotted, twitch-swinging, tongue and eyes strained from their running hutches, swollen, livid, engorged, I took leave of Lincoln with not a Jew in sight, and only the relishing lesser gentiles to herd me into Hell.

John de Lexinton's Tale

I would have been a fool not to have seen the possibilities. From the moment I heard the commotion in the street, the shouts of anger, the word "Jew" screeched into the night air as though Lincoln were overflown by cockatoos, from that moment I knew what to do. Choosing the least detrimental of alternatives has ever been my special talent. The fact of the matter is that only Little Hugh knows what really happened, and he is no longer what might be considered a material witness. So the field belonged to the nimblest. That my brother Henry is Bishop of Lincoln, successor to Holy Grosseteste, is witness to my, ah, agility. Brother Henry was hardly designed for the purple, ungraced, or shall I say unburdened, as he is by the weight of wit or intelligence. Still, he does have a pleasing face and a positively ecclesiastical smile, which two dependable steeds have many a chariot pulled to the stars. A few words in the royal ear . . . and presto! Fool into bishop.

Yet clearly an event was needed to distinguish what promised to be a most unremarkable episcopate. Thus it was that on the night of the first of August in the year 1255, when I looked out my window at the swarming crowd, I recognized the occasion at once. As God is my judge I wanted not the execution of the Jews! I wished only the confession, that the child might be acclaimed martyr, and installed in the cathedral. Lincoln would have its new saint. Alas, I had counted too much on the indifference of the English royalty. Henry III of England. Defender of the Faith, Keeper of Shrines. Faugh! There is never enough Mass for him. He must eat Body and drink Blood morning, noon, and night.

As for Beatrice, playing out the Mater Dolorosa, she cared not a fig for the brat. Oh, pardon me, Little Saint Hugh, whose sire, although he existed fully in the flesh (and in hers as well, I trow), exists not at all in her memory. To my knowledge she is but lately accorded the designation "widow," as is meet among all mothering whores who though they yet be whoring mothers find such a calling less than meet before priest and schoolmaster. For twenty-six days, unbratted Beatrice lay at house with not a murmur of discontent, visited (it is scarcely breathed) on three separate nights by a caftan, the beard of whom caught once the moonshine long enough to be seen by one whose pouch I have amply stuffed in the past. Doubtless Our Lady of Sorrows and the Jew examined well each other's treasure, exchanging gold for unsanctified viands. But trifling hearsay has become grand heresy. Such is the miracle of faith.

At last she roused from lidded greed, and prick'd, as it were, by a different lance, ambled to the Bailgate, where last the boy was seen, then down Steep Hill to Jewtown to lean on Copin's well, wherefrom radiated upward her son and her glory. It is, at the very least, curious that later, with the Jews imprisoned in the Tower, Beatrice came to me, aglow with her new piety, to plead for the release of one of them. From the fountain of her sorrow splashed the waters of forgiveness. For one Jew. Peitivin blackbeard, Peitivin rich, Peitivin night visitor. And, madam, what of the rest? Ah, let God's will be done. Only Peitivin then? So be it.

And what of the truth? Now, there is a matter, not of fact, but of taste and theater. As for me, I know only that the boy chose his playground not wisely, and fell or was pushed into the cesspool. Enticement by the Jewess was a deft touch. As for the sacrifice, no. It is known that the Jews perform their ritual murders at Passover, yet here is August. Well, no matter. I have a source, the Stuffed Pouch himself, which holds that the wretched boy tumbled into a cesspool in back of the Jew's house where he putrefied for the next twenty-six days, and then rose to the surface. You can imagine their dismay when they saw the little corpse floating there. Especially as the next day was the wedding of Benedick ben Moshe's daughter, Belaset, and the gentiles were certain to make trouble of some kind. Actually, the specter of the charge of Ritual Murder occurred to the Jews themselves before it did to anyone else. Thus they placed Hugh wellside in the house of Copin and hoped for the best. Bad luck.

How these Jews do stand in awe of rank and position. Even at his moment of direst peril, Copin loved my presence in his house.

Chaucer's Tale

'Tis charming, I own, this tale of Little Hugh slain by the Jews for his devotion to the Virgin, and of how She sustained him after death by Her powers, and caused "O Alma Redemptoris" to issue from his corpse. It is true, by Christ's blood. Not many more than one hundred years ago did such a boy ascend to heaven, as is well assured by writ and knowledge. It will please everyone to hear it again.

Jews? Truth to tell, I have never seen one. Yet who in England is not glad for their expulsion? How just that the blast which drove them from our shores grew from this child's last sigh. They are not gentle as we are.

We'll have this sweet tale, so apt for a pilgrimage, between the lechery of the Merchant's Wife and lily-pure Sir Topaz.

111

Somewhere in the middle. Well, now, shall it be the Monk who tells it? No . . . I'll save him for venery. The Lawyer? No, his work's more solemn. The Prioress? Yes, by all that is pious, the Prioress, and a fine joke it will be on my nuns of Saint Leonard. A worldly dame at that with a broad white brow and gray eyes. If she were not a Prioress . . . But enough . . . the venery is for the Monk. The Frustrated Mother is my theme, and Hugh's fair game for her, fleshless and hallowed, just the filling for that pie. Her name? Madame Eglantine, for the flower. Oh, that is good. Happiest of inspirations. I shall construe an elegant Eglantine, coy and simple, comme il faut, whose brow is like the sail of a trireme, and about whose arm coils a coral cobra Cleopatran. . . . Hold, Chaucer. Rein in. Decorative, yes, but decorous as well. Still, a worldly nun I'll have, with wit and beauty.

Pets she shall have, little hounds to wriggle in her lap, whom she doth feed with milk and roasted flesh, just the choicest firstlings of her dish, mind you, and over whose little corpses she doth mourn as for afflicted children. So charitable and piteous, she weepeth to see a dislocated mouse bleeding in a trap. Such is my lady Prioress who, with beauty bland and lifting voice, shall tell the tortures visited upon the Jews, how they were disjointed by pulling horses, and hanged from a cart.

She must swear once. That will be tasty. "By Saint Loy," she'll give a cry. Such a gentle curse does not twist the mouth to speak it. "Amor vincit omnia" is etched upon her brooch, which she fingers alternately with her beads. I'll leave unlit the sentiment here implied.

Oh, yes, the Jews. One must return to them. O cursed folk of Herod come again, of what avail your villainous intent? That'll do. Still, I am keenest to draw the lady. The courts and convents will read her knowingly, and with all good pleasure. She is familiar to my friends. The others, for the most part, cannot read.

All in all, it is a most felicitous joining, my nun of both worlds, and her child paradisiacal. And, ah, the Jews.

The Harbinger

Lucas had not touched her in twelve years. That wasn't so surprising, considering the fact that he was seventy-six years old. One summer he had quietly shriveled into retirement. No announcement, just a comfortable agreement with himself, she supposed. Ora had briefly wondered at the wisdom of nature and accepted without regret. They still shared the same bed, and now and then their legs would touch and she would feel the hairlessness of his calves. It made her sad. When she touched her own slack flesh or looked in the mirror at her dry gray hair, she felt no emotion. Only curiosity. It was "interesting" to watch age sift into her body. Such a tender invasion. But she hated to see Lucas get old. He needed his youth more than she did. A man does. It's the strength that matters to him. He's got to get up into a pear tree and saw off the dead branches. When he can't or it hurts too much to do it anymore, he gets quiet and stary. Still there was so much work to do on a fruit farm, even a small one, and they had no help. A hundred pear trees could sap a man's strength. Ora worried over him and his lunch and his boots.

They were two weeks into April and Ora was standing by the sink peeling onions. Work always absorbed her fully, so that the chill that crawled across the middle of her back came unemphatically to her attention. It merely eased across her mind. Her hands kept working but she half turned to see the shadow of a man disturbing the kitchen floor. It was another second before she realized it was Lucas. He was standing at the doorway looking at her.

"What you doin' back so soon, Lucas? It's not lunchtime."

For a long moment he hadn't answered, and she felt the severity of his gaze.

"See ya," he said, and slouched outside again.

Now that was odd, she had thought. It *was* odd, but Ora preferred not to think about it and did not again until much later.

That night, as she undressed, he raised up on one elbow and watched her. He had had yellow hair and white teeth; now the yellow was in the teeth and the hair was without any color at all. Thin and fine as a baby's. His pale blue eyes seemed always about to liquefy and run out of their sockets.

"Aren't you tired, Lucas? Here, get into your pajamas."

He did, and as she fell asleep she was almost sure that he was lying awake and tense. Ora awoke to feel his hand on her body. She had been dreaming of moths. In her dream she had gone up into the attic to put away the heavy winter coats. As she opened the old chest they flew out, a little white cloud, fluttering, staying close together, moving as one. They rose toward her face and she backed quickly away, her arms shielding her head. The moths floated closer. She was in a corner, half crouched, head upraised and her face covered with her arms when they settled on her, covering her eyes, sucking her lips, beating at her nostrils. They crept beneath the neck of her blouse and down her body, itching, crawling. With a groan she stirred and twisted herself awake.

It was then she felt Lucas' burry hand on her body. The knowledge of it startled her to motionlessness, and she lay with her back to him, frightened, unsure of what she should do, and not knowing, she lay still, submitting. After a while he stopped and she could feel his arm lying heavily on her and his breathing

115

told her that he was asleep. It was Ora who lay awake until dawn.

At daybreak she rose, dressed, and walked outside and up to the sloping orchard of pear trees in neat rows. The narrow black branches were still leafless and dry.

Luke's got a lot of lopping to do this year, she thought. She walked slowly up the slope to the further end of the orchard, out of sight of the house. The last tree in the next to the last row had been struck by lightning in the fall. She remembered hearing the crack, as of a large bone breaking in her ear. It was followed by a growl, black and ominous, that gathered in the deep chest of the sky and rose to be coughed from its running wet mouth. The storm had awakened her and she lay in bed thinking, So close, it's hit a tree. Next to her, Lucas had stirred and with a sudden movement turned and threw a leg across her thighs. He did not awaken. For a long while she lay imprisoned, then sat up and lifted the leg from her body and placed it gently on the bed. Then she rose and stood by the window, watching the rain, listening to the streams pouring from the eaves.

The next morning Lucas had gone out to see, and had reported to her the injured tree. The largest branch had been torn loose and lay on the ground, attached to the trunk by a small isthmus of bark. It wouldn't take much sawing to separate it completely. That was in November.

Now she paused by the tree, looking down at the fallen branch, submitting to the feeble spring sun. That sun gelded by the knives of winter sniffed about the crevices of earth, fingering her wrinkled face and blue-veined hands, and she let it, feeling no warmth from the cool rays, but hoping.

She had to think about Lucas, what he had done last night. It seemed surreptitious, furtive, almost boyish. She could understand why he didn't talk about it beforehand. He'd always been somewhat shy about their lovemaking, as though it were woman's work. He never talked about it, just did it, surely

116

enough, but shyly, too. Ora wouldn't have expected there to be any conversation about this. But what's got into him? she wondered. I'm frightened.

By the time she got back into the house she was thoroughly chilled. Lucas was boiling water for the coffee. They didn't speak of it.

"If it keeps up like this, we'll be in flower in three weeks, Luke."

"That's right. Gonna be a good year for pears."

"What's it gonna be today, Luke?"

"Checkin' and mendin' the fence. Probably take me all day, what with a lot of the big stones knocked out."

"Well, you wear your high boots and I'll bring lunch out and we can eat out by the trees."

At noon she took the basket of sandwiches and fruit up the hill and down the far slope. Lucas was far below, at the edge of the north field. The sun was pleasantly warm and she enjoyed the walk. When she had come to within fifty yards of where he stood, she could see that he wasn't working. He was standing still, his back to her, looking over the stone fence at the pasture beyond. She had a faint tremor of alarm, which passed as quickly as it had come, and she continued walking toward him. Immediately behind him she stopped and turned to follow his gaze. In the pasture beyond she saw the two horses, one mounted and high, rhythmically, relentlessly, its mane shaking with each probe, its head lowered and straining forward on the long curved neck. The other was docile, accepting, her head turned to the side as though waiting, waiting, on the brink. Once her hind legs buckled under his force, then, wobbling, stiffened to brace against him. Lucas was watching, absorbed, unaware of her presence, his whole body drawn to tightness and hung from those blinkless blue eyes.

"Lucas," she said quietly. Her throat was dry and she felt cold.

He did not turn or answer. She watched, too, but her gaze

turned from the pasture to Lucas and back again. There was a sudden loud, high, ringing neigh. The male's head shot up and back, eyes bulging with white, mane electrified, and the force of his body pushed the female forward in an awkward burst of side steps. She struggled to maintain her balance. Abruptly the stallion dropped from her back and bent immediately to nibble at the grass. His insolent tail flicked and whisked. The female remained still, hind legs apart. She seemed to be suffering his departure, or, heavy with the smear of life, unable to move. As they parted, Lucas gave a deep sigh, turned, and said:

"I'm hungry. Let's eat now."

That night he moved across her body gravely, recklessly, kneading her, pressing. He seemed occupied by something, a lust, late and suddenly sprung, that licked his blood and itched his flesh.

"Lucas?" she said. It was a question. Again, "Lucas?"

He did not answer, and his breathing came fast and hoarse. Now and then he coughed wetly. Arthritically ajar, she lay still as he poked among the dry leaves of her. In her hand she clutched a balled handkerchief and listened to an owl deriding the night.

The next day she mourned the purple bruises on her bony prominences, and remembered the clacking noises they made when bone struck bone. His struggle saddened her, the long slow swelling, the small puff of dry smoke. That was all there was. If only they could talk about it, but then, they never had, and surely not now. "No good will come of it," she whispered to herself. "It's not good."

It was unusually quiet at the farmhouse. For three weeks they circled each other during the day and played out their solemnities at night. Lucas' passion had sprung, not an old man's fancy but a dark ritualized thing, earnest, implacable. It needed no words and none were spoken. It was outside of themselves, living in the house, a weight, a goad. They faced each other at dinner with it seated between them. It needed no food. What they ate was somehow its food, fed it, and they grew thin and wordless.

She made her way up the slope with the lunch basket on her arm. The trees were in full bud but no open flowers yet. Who could imagine the hot color soon to be delivered from those cool knobs? When she reached the top she paused under the blasted tree, and from the shade of the tree next to it peered out into the brilliant vision-taking sunlight. It was hot as the edge of a knife. She saw it all happen as from within an airless rocking bubble. Lucas was in the pasture with the two horses. He had taken off his clothes and was standing naked beside the mare. He seemed to be studying her flanks, the fleshy rump. The stallion faced her, cheek by cheek. Their unstirred tails and manes hung heavily in the absolutely still air. For a long moment they were frozen in a group that was almost one-dimensional. Suddenly Lucas raised his hand to touch the mare's rump.

At that instant the stallion flung up and backward on his hind legs as though pulled at the neck by a powerful rope. His mane flashed and sprayed about his head and his great boxy teeth gaped at the sky. A scream broke from his mouth and bubbled out his nose as he galloped his forelegs down, down from their height, charging through the sunlight onto Lucas. At the last moment he turned and looked up at the rearing horse, but made no move to run or even to raise his arm to fend it off.

Ora heard the thud as the dented ground complained. Lucas never moved but lay where he was flung. Again and again the stallion rose, shook at the zenith, gathering, then raced down the burning air to smack his hoofs into the man. From the distance the hoofs were tiny. They swung delicately on the legs. All the while, the mare stood motionless, presenting her rump, staring down at the grass, only her ears pointing to listen. Ora leaned against the tree, her face fluttering downward. Spiking from the torn base, the blackened limb lay upon the ground; its dry little branches were covered with fierce, open blossoms.

A Blue
Ribbon Affair

Bertie pushed the back end of the stretcher down the long dark corridor of the ward. Small parabolas of orange light spread like moonlets over the black gape of each doorway they passed, marking but not illuminating the interiors, from each of which issued a special message for the brief train of passers-by: a little Hail and Farewell in the form of a hawk-spit, a belch, the country smell of flatus, or the rattling of phlegm in the unresisting throat. Some little memento to take with them to Brady. That's what the morgue was called. Everything in this hospital bore the name of a hoary donor who, decades ago, had given up his money and his ghost, the former in the hope of striking a bargain for the latter. Thus the morgue was called Brady. And there was Farnam, and Tompkins, and Dana, and Winchester. It was old Yankee money.

The right rear wheel of the stretcher squeaked gratingly all down the long hall until they stopped in front of the elevator. While they waited, Bertie went around to the side, and keeping his eyes averted from the mounding cargo, he kicked the wheel hard and sharply three times. The upper end of the body jiggled in response, and the sheet which had been covering the head slipped off, revealing the face through the open paper shroud.

What of the other? That one at the foot of stretcher, guiding it, steering with her light but powerful touch, sometimes rest-

121

ing no more than an index finger on the handle to maintain its direction? In the elevator he could see her fat smooth arms separated from the pudge of her hands by incredibly narrow wrists, no more than crevices in the fat, really, as though those arms were constricted by rubber bands. He gave a quick furtive glance downward and saw one stuffed and ample calf, narrowing suddenly to an isthmus of ankle that was recklessly delicate, then fanning into the tongue and laces of a crepe-soled oxford. For one instant he imagined her thighs, twin slopes rising, hung near the apex with symmetrical folds of pink and secret flesh. The picture flipped into his brain, sizzled there like a slide melting in a hot projector for an instant before he could click it off. His gaze tore guiltily from her and rested inadvertently on the corpse. It ricocheted from the face and bird-footed, at first tentatively, then with more assurance, onto a speck of bright blue ribbon, still tied in the gray thatch that sat like a fouled and empty last year's nest on top of her old-lady face. He hadn't meant to look at that face, ever, and only flight from incipient pubic woolgathering could have made him do it. Beneath the scraggle in which the little ribbon twinkled bravely, the genderless old features drooped as though a rubber Halloween mask had been tossed on the stretcher. The beak of the nose pointed down and almost into the dry fissure of the fallen mouth, unsupported by teeth. The partially closed eyelids revealed half-moons of soiled white. It was only the ribbon that identified it as belonging to one sex, Miss or Mrs. Somebody. Bertie had a feeling that the nose, lips, and ears could be broken off like pieces of slate, leaving the sphinxish defects of unearthed statuary. But that blue ribbon! He was drawn to it now. It was tied in a small bow and sat at the side of her head like a butterfly. The person who had tied it there could not have known that she was going to die and be brought down here. Surely it could not have been put on *after* she died! No, when it had been put in *someone* had hoped she would go on living, or expected her to keep on doing whatever it was she did—rasping out breath, discharging waste, raising her right hand to squeeze a finger on command. That person, the ribbon-tier, had unwittingly been decorating a dead-elect! It was probably a nurse, or her daughter, a sister perhaps. Would it shock her to think of it now? Shame her as though she had been discovered doing the silliest, stupidest thing?

Actually Bertie thought it was beautiful—very. The sight of it sitting there, reflecting the light, impossibly, arrogantly blue. It was enough to shine the eyes. With tears. The rest no longer moves (in either sense). It is unstirring and stirs not. It is interesting. But that ribbon is dear, thought Bertie, dearer than anything he had seen here over the months. He tried to think why. The defiance of it—the coming to full glory now, not before, but now, in that gray straw, breaking into bloom like an alpine flower between rocks—the heartbreaking cleanliness of it. I hope they won't take it off, thought Bertie. Maybe they'll leave it there and when it's done, finished, and the gutted hulk is reefed up with twine and bagged, it will still be there, twinkling in the darkness, winning.

"Well, here we are, the basement." The nurse had spoken. The sound of her voice startled him and seemed immensely inappropriate, like laughter in a graveyard. But it was not unmusical. She was thirty-five at least, but if he had not seen her, had only heard that voice, he would have pictured a much younger woman, a girl, even.

"I'm Joyce Renfrew."

It was as though this first remark were the herald of a rockslide of syllables which now tumbled from her mouth. She turned to smile at him, and her lipstick gleamed wetly. They had left the elevator and had started down the block-long service corridor to the morgue.

"I only work three nights a week. Just to keep my hand in. Don't want to forget how! You never know when you're going to have to go back to work again. You're Bertie, aren't you?"

"Yes. Bertie Shields."

"I haven't seen you before. But I've heard about you."

"Oh?" he asked.

"From one of the other girls. She thinks you're cute." Her laughter tripped up a scale of six notes.

"Oh, who?"

On the edge of his vision the blue bow bobbed with the motion of the stretcher.

"Never mind. Say, you're tall. How tall are you?"

"Six-two." He was distinctly uncomfortable.

There was a slight downward slope in the corridor, and taking advantage of it, she stepped to the side of the stretcher and waited to join him at the head. They were walking side by side.

"You play basketball?"

"I have."

"Where? Saint John's?"

He nodded.

"What year?"

"Second." He strained his eyes to see the door at the end of the hall.

"Oh, really? What are you going in for?"

"I don't know yet."

"You want to be a doctor?" She was close now and her bare upper arm brushed his. It was cool as a smooth stone! He quickened his pace, pushing harder on the stretcher and taking long strides.

"Hey! What's the hurry? She isn't going anyplace. And neither am I," she added, as an afterthought. "Slow down." She rested her hand on the stretcher as though to restrain it. He saw where the gold wedding ring bit deeply into the third finger, saw how the flesh around it rose up to enfold it, draw it in, devour it. She was close now. There were little abuttings, touchings, at each step, now at the shoulders, now at the feet. She was holding the handle so that her little finger rested carelessly on his thumb. He lifted his hand to his neck and scratched ostentatiously, then let it back down at a safe distance from hers. Scarcely had he grasped the handle when he felt her hand settle onto his. He thought his knuckles must be poker-hot and burning her palm. She had soft palms.

Oh, God, thought Bertie. Let's hurry up and get to the morgue and back again. He licked the salt sweat from his upper lip.

"What did she die of?" he asked, a touch of desperation cracking his voice.

She shrugged. "Does it matter? Nobody gets off the planet alive, that's all I know. You only go this way once, right, Bertie? Better make the most of it."

With relief bordering on nausea he saw the letters on the corrugated opaque glass of the door: MORGUE.

"Here," he said, sidling neatly away. "I've got the key."

He fumbled with the lock, opened the door inward, and set the doorstop to hold it open. He flicked on the wall switch and the room burst into a fluorescent glare. She was still at the head and he pulled the foot of the stretcher in through the doorway. As she entered she turned sideways as though to make room for the passage, and with a deft kick of her heel released the doorstop, causing the heavy door to fold slowly, gassily shut. There was a liquid finality to the click as the lock engaged itself. Bertie's heart slammed into his ribs at the sound. He moved toward the built-in stacks of refrigerators at the opposite end of the room, guiding the stretcher between the rows of autopsy tables. The smell of formaldehyde was cold and heavy; it had a decongesting effect for which he was immediately grateful.

"Here, let's try this one," he said and, turning the heavy handle of one of the metal doors, pulled it. A pair of skinny white feet, soles first, presented themselves at the open door. He quickly slammed it shut.

"No room at the inn." She laughed. "Try that one." She pointed to another door. He pulled it open.

"See?" she said triumphantly. "Empty. I'm a good guesser, Bertie."

He drew out the long metal tray on rollers to its full length, stepped back and to the right side of the stretcher, and with a graceful movement reached under the body, his left arm beneath the shoulders, the right under the knees. It was shockingly light, as though already much of its substance had moldered away. In a movement that was not without tenderness, he carried the body to the tray and placed it gently down, then slid the tray home. The last thing he saw as it disappeared into the dark recess was the winky blue . . . "Oops!" As the door clanged shut he felt her hand on his buttocks and leaped like a flushed bird. The hand maintained its contact, as if possessed of a mucilaginous power. Abruptly he felt it sliding around his hip toward the very bottom of his abdomen. Then the fingers, dipping, inexorable.

"What's this?" Her voice was infinitely coy, practiced. Bertie felt his trapped penis struggling erect. She drew him, he let her, toward the stretcher, then turned with her back to it and with an agile little movement raised herself with her arms. Again her hand was in contact, this time grasping the buckle of his belt. She lay back on the stretcher, pulling him close.

"Get up on it," she whispered.

"On the stretcher?" He was incredulous.

"Yes." She nodded. "It's comfortable."

Her arm drew his head down. He did not remember throwing one leg over the stretcher and climbing on, but he did see her face close beneath his, and her mouth open as at the beginning of a small scream, just before he kissed it.

A Pot of Ivy

In a hospital bed a young man lies. He is motionless. It is a hot day and he is wearing only a pair of madras shorts which are several sizes too big for him. From the fly of his shorts a brown rubber tube leads into a larger plastic one. This droops sinuously over the side of the bed and into a plastic bag. Now and then a column of urine will surge down the tube and disappear over the edge. He watches as though it were a silent movie. It seems miraculous that urine should still form somewhere in his body, to be let out through that fly. Suddenly he turns his head. The movement is in contrast to the absolute stillness of the rest of him. It is shocking. He seems to be staring out the window but really he is looking at the window ledge, where there is a flower-pot full of grape ivy. The plant is exuberant, gleaming. Its tendrils grasp the ledge and leap at the pane.

"Die, plant," he whispers.

The young man's name is Chester. He is driving along the coast. His young wife, Anita, sits beside him. He can see, out of the corner of his right eye, her yellow hair against the ultramarine blue sea.

"I'm so hot, aren't you?"

He nods.

"Chester. Let's stop for a swim."

"Soon."

"Right now. Okay? It's deserted here. We can put on our bathing suits right here in the car and have a cool dip. I've got to."

He is already pulling the car off to the side and well up on a shoulder of the road. They undress. He reaches over to cup her breast with his hand.

"Unh, unh, too hot." She gives him a regretful smile.

They run toward the rocks at the edge of the water, pause for a moment suspended between the two elements, then plunge in. Chester is a strong swimmer and plows straight out to a protruding rock. He clambers up and stands there. He is very beautiful standing in the sea watching her. When she is almost there, then climbing up, he whips around and dives from the opposite side. Now it is Anita who stands in the sea, her long yellow hair sculpted by the water. But something is wrong. There is a hoarse bubbling cry. She is bending forward. A wonder comes over her face. Her hand flutters to her mouth, back side to. Chester is hurt, he is drowning. There is a crushing impact to the top of his head. (Horror!) He cannot feel or move his body, any part of it, only his head. It is like becoming unplugged from life. He is only his head bobbing in the water. There is the moment when he even feels in his face the tiny aura of having "given," the way a bough, bent by the wind, gives when its tensile strength is exceeded.

The girl jumps into the water and closes upon him; her thin arm encircles his chest from the side and propels him toward the rock. Chester is clear of the water, choking against the cold stone. Barnacles graze his cheek. She is sobbing and breathless. From inside the ambulance he hears the siren rise and fall. It is a sickening sound. He feels catapulted.

In the hospital room, Anita is standing by the window. She is cool and calm. He watches her place the flowerpot in the center of the window ledge, fingering the vine, arranging it.

"There!" she says to the plant. "Wave to your new roommate.

Hope you two get on well. How do you like it?"

"Fine. Fine. Very nice." He wishes she would go. Embarrassing to have her see him paralyzed, all the sturdiness gone like a mist that's evaporated. Finally she goes. Her visits grow shorter and shorter, more and more silent, until without any good-byes (thank God) she is gone. Chester feels bereft and relieved.

Now he lies in his bed with a canvas traction sling under his chin, pulled by weights at the head of the bed. Now and then he raises his head and looks down at the rest that he cannot feel. It looks like a white waste, with here and there a swatch of black hair like burnt-out scrub. What he feels most like is a candle: white, dead wax, only his head, the flame, alive. Most of the time he is thinking how to snuff it. Once again he turns his head to look at the plant. The muscles of his neck have grown strong. They are columns, pillars. The ivy, too, is flourishing, powerful. Chester falls asleep and dreams that lithe, strong vines have grown from his shoulders, winding around his arms, coiling about the wrists and fingers. Shoots slide across his chest and down between his legs. Wherever it lies upon him, he can feel its coldness.

"Feel! Oh, God!" His eyes spring open.

A nurse comes into the room.

"Time to turn, Chester," she says. She rolls him up on his side. Bending one of his knees and propping pillows against his back, she adjusts his chin strap. "There. That comfortable? Want to read?"

He shakes his head, but she puts a magazine on the music stand by the side of the bed. It opens to a double page of writing, no pictures.

"That will last longer," she says. "I'll be back soon."

Chester is up to something. As soon as she leaves he begins. He is bobbing his head, at first tentatively, even feebly, but then, feeling the rhythm, he thrusts harder and harder, pulling back to the limit, then throwing forward as hard as he can. With each jerk he sees his shoulders and chest move forward, then fall back. It is very tiring, and he grits his teeth and grunts with each excursion. Finally he stops and waits for the nurse to come back.

"I need to be over more," he says.

"Not too much or you'll fall. There isn't a lot of room." But she pulls him over further, tipping him a bit forward. "O.K.?"

"A little more. There, I can see fine now."

"Don't fall." She smiles. "Turn the page?"

"Please."

She leaves, and Chester cannot wait to start again. Now he is into it fully, pull and thrust, pull and thrust. He can see his shoulders moving. She will be back in ten minutes. Pull and thrust, pull and thrust. He is sweating, panting. Five minutes to go! There is desperation on his face. His heart is plunging and wheeling like a hawk, but he cannot feel it. Look! His body is leaning forward. It is at forty-five degrees. Again and again, straining, quivering, to get the last bit of good from each one. His eyes are open and he can see the window, a black square, swinging and rocking crazily, and on the ledge the ivy menacing the curtain. Faster, faster! and then he stops. He stops and knows it is done. He is going to fall. His body is hung precariously over the edge at an angle which, if scarcely exceeded, will make him fall. He moves his head to slip the chin strap to a lower position about his neck. Then Chester heaves one final time. He feels himself hang for an instant over the edge, then flop. There is a thud as his legs hit the floor. His arms swing limply. He waits the long moment for the strap to jerk against his throat. He cannot breathe, nor does he try. He is like a doll thrown across the room by a child.

An Act of Faith

Faith never expected to fall. Not past that smile, those wings. The thought never occurred to her. She did, though. Slipped from his neck, her slow cheek sliding down his body, over the strong chest, the abdomen corrugated with muscle, twining the thighs with her thin white arms. When at last, still drowsy, her fingertips lingered at, then left his heel, she gazed back along the upspringing dizzy building and saw against the sky the bright cloak of his wings settling about him. Then it was she had an instant of utter fulfillment, of absolute joy, her first, when she thought it would be perfectly all right to die.

Even now Faith could have laughed at how she thought he was a window washer at first, had completely misinterpreted the whole thing. She thought it showed a certain unfortunate limitation of the spirit. That was before the Grace came, or whatever it was that leaped like a deer deep within her, moving in the quietest, most forestial parts of her, and changed her forever. Then she was able in a flash to *see* him for what he was, and herself for what she might become. It still hurt to laugh. All the ribs on the left broken, they said. She landed on her left side, one arm cushioning her head, her knees bent, the way she always slept. All she could manage was a smile, which she did quite a lot of now when the nurses weren't there to see. Once she had grinned, quite openly, she knew, when the doctor had told her that no one could fall eight stories and survive without a miracle. "Well?" she wanted to say, her voice arch with implication. "Well?" And let him just think that one over for a while.

Looking back on it, a more perceptive person might have guessed at the possibilities. There was something in the air that morning, a stillness, as though the earth were expecting a visitor. It had just finished raining all night, and, as if to make up for it, the sun had broken open like a ripe melon, spilling its very brightest sunshine like seeds. She had heard a brushing at the window and, turning, saw him outside. He smiled, and raised his hand to wave. Before she could stop herself she had smiled and waved back. When she realized what she had done, actually *encouraged* a man at her window who had been peeping in at her for God knows how long while she slept wearing only a thin summer nightgown that you could see through, and him with his shirt off—well, she almost died. But it was too late to take it back, and in a strange way, she didn't want to.

Even after she turned away she could see his dark Mediterranean face and curly black hair, the smile-parted lips presenting his perfect teeth for the sun to reflect upon. She had at once decided that it was the most beautiful face she had ever seen in all her thirty-two years. Candor, that's what it had, and something a bit more than affection, which should have been downright shocking to her, but didn't faze her at all, as though every window washer should gaze with affection at the people on the other side of the panes.

But then she realized that she couldn't just stand there. She had to make her breakfast and get off to the store. Mr. Nagle docked latecomers, and made snide, vaguely threatening remarks, and jobs were hard to come by. Well, that was certainly all over. Finished in a blaze of glory, as they say. But at the time it *did* seem that she had to get there and not be late. One cannot change the habits of a lifetime overnight. It wasn't her fault that she had been whisked right out of business school into the back office of Nagle's Furniture Store, as though delivered there blindfolded and gagged by an armored car. Speeding into spinsterhood. It was this city. Such a cold, impersonal, cruel place that sucked the life out of its children, and then discarded its adults as empty shells.

Now of course she was glad she had stayed as she was, that is, untouched, pure, until that day. In one moment she had made up for all the grayness that had gone before. She had caught up with and gone whizzing by those others she had listened to with slowly mounting panic. All that talk about husbands, babies, houses, and "good times." He had quite simply come to her window and welcomed her, and she had gone to him, and he had healed her or whatever you want to call it. In a single moment she had recovered from her life. That was it! Her whole life had been a terrible sickness—she saw that now so clearly—and he had cured her of it. Now she saw that it had all been on purpose, that she wasn't meant to bloom until thirty-two years had passed. After all, there were plants that took a hundred years.

She could not have explained the certainty that came over her, the serenity she felt when she turned again to face the window. She wasn't sure, when she started toward him, whether it was to ask him to come in or what, but something told her that he wouldn't come, would just hover there outside the window smiling and welcoming her. When she got to the window she saw that what she thought was clothing or something wasn't. It was wings. Great luminous wings raised up, arching from his upper back in twin coils of muscle to unfurl into that radiant spread, that glory of feathers, pearly gray with fluttering silver tips. He was nodding to her, inviting her with his shining eyes, his raised brows, the turn of his head, the curve of his lip, the pillar of his neck, the lift of his arms, the whisper of his wings.

She stepped to the window and opened it wide. By now she was not at all surprised that there was no safety belt, no pail, brush, or sponge, no water. She felt graceful, aware of her body like a dancer, as she bent to climb out on the ledge. He moved then to place himself directly in front of her and a little lower, as if to guard her, to protect and reassure her. Faith stood on the ledge for a long time, gazing down, worshiping. Her room seemed to have receded to a distant place. There was only this outside, and *him*. She never thought of going back.

Slowly and powerfully she felt an urge rising in her to close with him, to lie against him, be enfolded by those wings. Oh, what must they feel like? At that moment she was insubstantial. Sunlight and air were flowing through her. She saw herself as beautiful, or rather, growing in beauty to match his. With her gaze never faltering, and with a movement so slow as to be at first imperceptible, she leaned, drifted, was taken against him, inhaled by him. Forever would she remember the heat beneath those wings. No matter how cold she was ever to grow, she would be warmed by the memory of it. And the stirring of the angel against her.

Lavinia
Armbruster

"But, Lavinia, what *shall* you do?"

"Do? Do? I shall treat this entire affair with the contempt that it so richly deserves."

Lavinia's nostrils were her most beautiful feature. Everyone said that. Narrow and finely carved, they were capable of the most immediate and passionate response. Like the sense organs of certain highly developed animals, they preceded her through life, their tiny vibrissae erect, bristling, and all but prehensile. One was never left in doubt with Lavinia. Where others blushed or perspired, Lavinia dilated or compressed. At the moment they were pulsating rapidly, expanding and contracting with a tautness that could mean but one thing: outrage.

"Hector's capacity for swinishness is without limit," she said, "and it is best that I have discovered this now before I should have made a disastrous error."

"Oh, yes, of course," murmured Nora. "He behaved the perfect pig, did he not?"

"Pig indeed! Wild boar would be more apt."

"But what of Mummadear?" moaned Nora. "She has been so counting on your marriage into the Savigny-Crespi line. With our own fortunes at ebb tide, Lavinia, it has been Mummadear's fondest hope that your *liaison* with the scion of that clan . . . "

"Are you suggesting, Nora? Are you suggesting that I might

135

be *sold* like a slave, a harem girl, to secure the position of my family?" Lavinia's nostrils puffed into full billow and remained there as she surveyed Nora's discomfort. When no answer was forthcoming, she threw her voice box into a dangerously deep contralto and quavered, "Never! Never shall I place at the disposal of such a beast my beautiful white body. I have too much respect for the memory of *Grand-père*. We *are* the issue of the Earl of Dover, after all. That much at least is immutable, thank God."

"Darling best sister," wept Nora, "be not overmuch in tumult. It jeopardizes the complexion, and see now, one of your combs has come loose."

"Oh? Which one?"

"The tortoise shell with seed pearls."

Lavinia slowly arched one alabaster arm upward to her coiffure, pressing the dislocated comb deeply back into the polished masses of her hair.

"This must stop." She breathed heavily. "I shall not be thus undone by him. Even *in absentia* he contrives to rob me of my dignity. Is it straight now, Nora?"

"Yes, sister, all is well again. What are we to do with Mummadear? She lies upon the ottoman, the Turkish, in a state of utter carelessness, her gown, the gray taffeta, unfolded at the hem, with a portrait of Father clutched in her hand, and giving rise to the most piteous sighs. I fear she may fall into a dwindle."

"I shall go to her. She must see that the events of that evening were a blessing in disguise, that in fact we have been saved by no less than the hand of Divine Providence from a great calamity."

"Do, do go to her. It will be such a comfort."

"And now, Nora, I wish to be alone. Perhaps solitude will award me the means to recapture my serenity."

Lavinia turned away and waited until she heard the rustle of her sister's afternoon dress of green shantung as it brushed the

136

doorway at the opposite end of the library. Alone, she gazed about at the shelves of books, each one bound in leather and tooled in gold. Although she had read none of them, their very presence was a comfort to her, as though she were the living symbol of every tragic figure on those pages. Impulsively she raced toward the divan in a burst of tiny precipitous steps and flung herself upon the black velvet cushions. She looked her best against black velvet, her moon-colored skin creaming the sable. There was never enough velvet in the house to suit her.

Lavinia pulled the combs from her hair with a sudden movement which gave a physical reality to an anguish which had hitherto been an abstraction. With the length of her hair cascading over the sofa and her head itself partially hung over the edge of the seat, she stared up at the ceiling, where a covey of cherubim flew in a circle, gauzy scarves mischievously fluttering between their thighs and quite incidentally concealing from view their pink and perfect improprieties. Within minutes the tears which had gathered in the corners of her eyes welled across the lids, and were streaming toward those matchless nostrils in two silver rivulets as like each other as the antlers of a buck.

"How could you, Hector?" she murmured to the prettiest cherub, whose fluffy buttocks repeated the overblown lines of a nearby cloud. "How could you?" The winged creature ignored her grief as though it were a mass of carnified indifference.

Lavinia sighed and turned to arrange herself upon the cushions as Odalisque; not the Manet, ample to the point of vulgarity, but rather the melancholy Ingres. She closed her eyes and saw once again the ballroom of Hollingsworth, that ballroom she had entered one months-ago evening with nothing weightier upon her bosom than the imminence of her betrothal, the announcement of which was due at exactly quarter to nine with a fanfare from the violins and woodwinds. Who

137

would have foreseen that she was to leave that room an insulted woman? She had danced with Sir Trevor, Lord Ashley, and the French *chargé d'affaires*, a little frog of a person whom Hector had referred to as *le petit fromage*. All the while she glanced unobtrusively about for a glimpse of Hector. That he was nowhere to be seen she attributed to his puckish penchant for provocation. He wished to appear only at the last instant to make a ringing declaration. But of course, she had thought, making an indulgent *moue* over the shoulder of the Frenchman, he *must* be *outré*. Nothing else would do for Hector. Still, how she would have loved to exchange one knowing glance with him.

At last the hour had arrived. Mummadear was beaming brilliantly in slow semicircles, and Nora, poor Norita, no longer able to contain herself in the waltz, was leaning upon her partner, Marshal Oberlin, in a manner that Lavinia would at any other time have considered *declassé*, but which she knew was entirely due to her darling sister's transport. Nonetheless Lavinia had made a brief mental note to admonish the dear for her lack of restraint, especially as the delighted Marshal was quite obviously in possession of indecorous thoughts.

The fanfare broke softly upon the evening air in terraced waves, and the figures in the ivory and gold ballroom drifted to stillness like the captured loiterers of Fragonard. A silence followed the dying strains of the music. No Hector. Once again the music. How annoying that the dolt of a conductor could not have played a different piece but must accentuate the awkwardness by insisting upon the same silly thing. Lavinia had at once decided that she loathed that hideous tinkling cantilena.

At the completion of the fourth rendition of *"Ouvre tes yeux bleus"* and just before Mummadear was to have fallen senseless to the parqueted floor, there was the most unseemly smash of glass and stamp of boot. The French doors flew open and Lavinia was quite sure that she never wished to see again a sight so horrendous, so unrelentingly ugly in all of its contours, as burst from the veranda into that ballroom. "Hector," she had gasped into the *chargé's* ear. For it was, must have been, he who stood there like some spangled satyr, grinning wickedly and in a state of cloven-footed dishevelment so utter that it could have been none other than the costume of madness. The sight of those white trousers open (yes, open!) and smeared with wine, mud, and heaven knew what further beastly excrescencies, and that coat from which the medals winked lewdly in the light of the great chandeliers, likewise open to reveal a broad expanse of shirt, if you please—this sight sent steel knives shooting across her brain, lancinating her to insensibility. So that when Hector, having found her in the crowd, had swayed drunkenly in her direction, she was totally unable to turn and flee, much less to speak the words that would terminate their relationship, but had remained quite planted to the dance floor in the suffocating grip both of her horror and of the Baron de Rochefoucauld, number six on her dance card. "Lavvy," roared Hector, "I've come to frighten ye wi' me trouser worm." This said with the most atrocious cockney leer, at which point, as though conducted to do so by the orchestral baton, Lavinia, Nora, and Mummadear sank into a family coma and knew no more.

The entire business lasted no more than three minutes but was like a burn which, though instantaneously incurred, yields scars enough to last a lifetime. She could not recall the means by which she departed that ballroom, although even now those hundreds of eyes remained embedded in her flesh.

Oh, Hector, Hector. How little you have understood me. Thirst explains me. And such a thirst as will ne'er be slaked save by the wine of you. Lavinia rose from the divan, Violetta now, a pallor of doom emblanching her cheeks, and floated toward the fruitwood secretary. Feverishly she unlocked her diary and wrote verbatim the words she had just addressed to the seraph above her. It was too touching a lament to consign to transience. It bore rereading through a lifetime of quiet regret and, one could hope, resignation, perhaps in moments snatched from her duties as governess on some high family estate.

It was all Mummadear's fault. She had complained all winter that her bowels were failing, and that the wherewithal simply *must* be found to take the waters in the summer, even if it meant that the topaz must be sold. Lavinia had sighed at the thought of losing the topaz, and tears had burbled from Nora's eyes as a vision of her mother appeared before her, her mother minus the giant orange stone impacted in her bosom. That lavaliere was the very cornerstone of her life. As a child she had laid her little tow head upon that brocade bust and peered into the topaz, deep, deeper, and deepest, seeing within its facets a world of ballrooms, spas, and candelabra reflected in polished wood. Oh, not the topaz, she had wept.

"But my bowels, Nora," Mummadear had said. "We must place the proper emphasis." Mummadear had a quaint style of phrasing that she had learned from Poppers when he was active in Parly. Of course now things were different, and affairs had straitened, as Mummadear had put it, leaving her and her two darlings with barely enough to put a face on in Society, what with the cost of silk and rouge, to say nothing of a carriage.

That was all Poppers' fault, Mummadear had said after she had discovered that he had behaved indiscreetly in France with the family moneys, and had capped it by "passing on" in some dreadful place in the Quartier Latin at the *établissement* of two aging froufrous from whom Mummadear had had to *purchase*, if you please, his remains in order to have them reinterred with a semblance of respectability in England. For six months the woman had taken to her bedchamber, where she sulked and loitered, wearing none of her pretty things, but entombed in maroon bombazine like some old Parisian concierge. It was during this period that her bowels first failed and, forever after,

140

she had implied to the girls that their father had done it to her by his carelessness.

At long last she had allowed herself to be swayed by the blandishments and tears of Nora and Lavinia, and at a small *soirée* made her reentry into Society, to which state she clung with all the toe-scrabbling tenacity of a Sherpa. It was the very next summer that they had gone to Cheltenham for the waters, and it was the very first day that Lavinia had met Hector. The walks and gardens were exquisite with moss and vines on the old stone. The pump room was a hive of social to and fro from lunch on into the evening. And at night there were the balls at each of the larger hotels. Circulation from one to the other was freely encouraged and as a consequence the walks were pleasantly alive with saunterers carrying fans and parasols and the other *accoutrements* of country idleness. Spirits were dangerously high. Mummadear attributed it to the waters, averring over and over again that the salubrity of one's bowels most certainly affected the general frame of mind. Lavinia could not abide the nasty stuff and, after one or two dutiful sips on the first day, tenaciously abstained.

"I do not share Mummadear's penchant for the waters," she said. "I find the odor unpalatably sulfurous."

"Nor I," said Nora, who carried a lavender sachet at her waist to fend off the stench. "Just see how the old dear swills from dawn to dusk."

But that was long ago and far away from the library where Lavinia lay, her honor soiled. Ah, Cheltenham, she cried to the heavenly host, birthplace of catastrophe. Would I had never drunk thy waters, felt the bite of thy sulfurous fumes. From thy pampered parks and walkways I have come to dwell in eternal sulfur, gagging, retching at the sheer unpalatability of life.

At first, she had but little understood the manner in which Hector came to stand at her side there on that summer day among the ferns of the glass-domed pump room. Now she knew full well that it was the unforgivable machinations of Mummadear, who urged the meeting upon the Duchesse de Savigny-Crespi, a quite ordinary woman upon whom the burden of uncounted wealth had been thrust. This luckless person was to spend the remainder of her life in a state of undisguised amazement. Totally lacking in manners or presence, she is unable to conceal her fundamental awkwardness in the halls and parlors of the aristocracy. After all, it is hardly unknown that it was through the whimsical legacy of a rich *roué* for whom the Duchesse was the grand obsession that she came to her present high station, now cemented forever by that most absurd of *liaisons*, her marriage to Edgare, Duc de Savigny-Crespi.

Mummadear, shortly before the journey to Cheltenham, had met in secret conclave with Hector's mother and had persuaded her that the means by which she could elevate herself to a state of permanent comfort in Society lay in the marriage of her son to a beautiful girl to whom the manners of Society came as naturally as the blush to her cheek. In brief, Lavinia Armbruster. The Duchesse, after some hesitation founded on the suspicion that Mummadear, like innumerable *grandes dames* before her, was in fact making overtures to her fortune rather than to her son, fell eagerly into the plot when she was presented with the notion that the compassionate and highborn Lavinia would, patient as a nun, devote herself single-mindedly to the social aggrandizement of her mother-in-law.

Thus was Lavinia led unsuspecting to the pump room at Cheltenham on the twelfth of July in the year 1882 to stand face to face with her destiny, holding in her hand nothing more than a glass of turbid water having the distinct odor of rotten eggs. It might well have been an omen, a warning, coded and subtle, sent from the lord of those regions where the affairs of love are managed.

"Lavinia Armbruster, I presume," he had begun.

"Yes, and you?" Her heart was even then palpitating at the sight of him, the stitching of his glove, the cut of his waistcoat. Even then she had thought him a *boulevardier* of the most pronounced type, and with a list of conquests as long as Don Giovanni's *mille e tre*. But it was undeniable that at that moment Lavinia had also fallen hopelessly, irrevocably in love.

Lavinia drew herself to a sitting position on the divan *à la* Madame Recamier and surveyed the wreckage of her life. In retrospect she ought to have sensed that there was something not a little Hungarian about Hector. A lack of bridle here, a certain heftiness of the tongue there; subtle, yes, but to a woman of her refinement and perspicacity no more than should have been immediately apparent. Lavinia reproached herself for having been obtuse, or at least *naïve*. Not that she liked preciosity in a man. No. A familiarity with horses, and other beasts, good brandy in his glass, good leather on his feet and (in this she considered herself dangerously *moderne*) a whiff of "experience"—these were no more than the ingredients of Manly Grace. No gentleman could ever be seduced to perpetuate his carefree ways in a life of license. Breeding would always prevail, and he would be drawn back to manor and title, the eternal verities, after all.

"Wherefore wert thou, sybarite? The hateful music swelling, the women *décolletées d'une façon outrageuse*, and everywhere the glitter of jewels and eyes, and I limp upon the shoulder of the Frenchman ('twas the scent of his pomade fierce and thick that I was to take with me from that ballroom, my senses forever made fast by mucilaginous tentacles of smell)."

With an enormous effort, Lavinia rose from the velvet divan to stand by the window. London is all mud, she thought, and the season is over. Faugh! What a disgusting spectacle it is. Bitter as the apples of Sodom! She did not turn at the sound of the library door clicking open. It was Nora. She could tell by the susurration of her green shantung gown, bouffant enough to brush with sound the marble pillars on either side of the doorway.

"Ah, Lavinia, do let's have a stroll 'neath the lime trees. They catch and hold the breeze admirably. And besides, you shall look sublime in orchid under a canopy of green. Ha ha ha." Her laughter twinkled in little bursts of celestial energy.

Lavinia remained gazing out the window, permitting the tiniest of wan smiles to spirit across her face, and then vanish.

"Nora, Nora, pet. What know you of passion and lorn? May you retain your innocence forever."

Turning now, she faced her sister. "I say, do you believe in the transmigration of souls?" Before the startled girl could respond, Lavinia went on. "In my next life I would be perfect and momentary. It is the *durability* of life that I find so trying, in fact utterly impossible. How much better to appear for a single ravishing instant, and then vanish, never to be recalled."

"But as what would you next appear?"

"As what, you ask, child. As what." The deepest of sighs let from her lips like the loosing of her very soul. "As a puff of wind on a hilltop, a warm and fleeting rain, the ultimate flight of a colored moth, the spume of a single wave. And in whatever guise, to blow, moisten, brush, or splash my Hector, and then be gone."

"I should sooner return as a body louse in the vicinity of his neck," said Nora, with impatience in her voice. "No man is worth the torment you are enduring. Why, you might as well go on a penitential retreat with a case of little whips and a bag of thorns. You did him no wrong. It is he should be made to suffer, be called to account. And now, sister, I shall be severe with you. I was never intended for a *garde-malade*. I do not give a tittle for any man's affections. You shall either rouse yourself from this elegiac mood or I shall petition Mummadear to send you to take the cure in some unspeakable place like

Germany. And you know very well that no one is going to Wiesbaden this year."

Lavinia gasped. Really the child was too bold. "It is I will petition Mummadear with reference to the incarceration of your tongue. Perhaps we can arrange to have it pierced in some colorful African fashion."

"Oh, let's not quarrel, sister dear," said Nora, embracing Lavinia briefly. "I care too much about your peace of mind, and it makes me spiteful."

"All right, pettikins," breathed Lavinia. "We'll promenade then, particularly since I must escape the sound of that pianola in the music room. It is being played all too cleverly."

They had walked barely half the length of the lime tree avenue when a man's voice rode in on the breeze. "I say, are parakeets in season? Or is it birds of paradise?" With a steely discipline that can only have been acquired in the drawing rooms of English society, and which might be the envy of the Queen's own regiment, the brace of Armbrusters sailed on without the slightest *frisson* of acknowledgment. When they had come out of earshot, it was Lavinia who spoke first.

"Effrontery," she hissed, then, after a pause, "Nora, did you get a look at him?"

"Heavens no. Why ever should I have?"

"There was something familiar about that voice. I have heard those tones in another time, another place."

"Never mind. To look now is out of the question. His footsteps are scarcely three paces behind us and, to be sure, he is pursuing in a reckless manner."

"Turn and see, Nora."

"I? Never."

"Then shall I," said Lavinia, answering the call of some awakening spirit within her. With that she came to a sudden and full halt, and turned quite completely about. There must be no suggestion of subterfuge or surreption. Treat brazenness with its reflection. The quickness of her stop and turn brought her face to face and within an inch of touching none other than (be still, heart!) Hector Alain de Savigny-Crespi, who at that moment was actually smiling at her!

"Nora," said Lavinia in a voice held at the middle range and without the slightest tremolo. "Lead me to a bench. I would sit."

"Allow me the honor," said Hector, still with the same mindless smile sloshed upon his face like a pail of slops.

"Go, lout," said Lavinia in the same even tone. At that the smile evaporated and it was Hector Penitent who stood there, remorseful, rich, pleading with his eyes. Lavinia's resolve shook momentarily. "I have surfeit of the human race, sir. Have the decency to abandon this pursuit."

"Never, until I have won from you the words I most long to hear: 'I forgive.' "

"That shall you never hear from my lips," she said, noticing how his own glistened with moisture.

"But let me speak, I implore you."

A wave of feeling took hold of the elder Armbruster girl, starting from her toes and billowing upward until her entire body was permeated with the most utterly transcendental sensation. Lavinia recognized it at once for what it was. Triumph.

"Nora?" said Lavinia. It was not a question nor an appeal, but rather a command similar to that given a servant or a child when his presence is no longer desired. Nora understood at once and, gathering handfuls of green shantung, she swept away as rapidly as decorum would permit. No sooner had she made her departure than Hector spoke.

"Brilliant coloring, what?"

"I beg your pardon?"

"The foliage. There are at least twelve shades of green here, although several are sufficiently subtle to . . ."

146

"How dare you, sir, intrude upon my misery. Have done. This confrontation threatens my very life."

"Then you *have* missed me," cried Hector. "Ah, sweet girl, that I have brought you unhappiness and shame I well know. It is to pledge to you my unwavering consolation that I have presumed to approach you once more. Know that it is my sole ambition to render you serene."

"Your ambition? Sir, although I smile now do not mistake it for acquiescence. I loathe you. What is your intention?"

"Believe that I wished to marry you. That having been accomplished, I should have bestowed upon you and your family the largesse and goodly things that you and you alone are capable of acknowledging. It remains my everlasting wish."

Lavinia felt a sudden urge to tears, but conquered it with great effort. There was something about this offer that could not but pluck her deepest chords. After all, the man was offering her his life, his money! Lavinia recognized this moment as the most important of her life.

"I shall never marry you, Hector. Not even the coronet of a vicomtesse embroidered in the corners of my handkerchiefs could console me for a life not worth living."

"Lavinia," he murmured in a voice that penetrated her armor with the suddenness of a hurled lance. The word was like a moan. "Lavinia." Again he spoke, and she whose name had thus been uttered felt as though a plume had been drawn across her bare abdomen.

"But hear me out or I"—and here he slumped upon the bench in the manner of young Werther in his sorrows—"or I shall put an end to a tortured life."

Lavinia Armbruster's cheeks flushed on either side of nostrils that fluttered helplessly before the abjection of her lover. He was hers! Her weeks of shame and pain were as naught beside the tragic, kingly (yes, she had to admit it: Hector's suffering was in the grand, the royal style) anguish of the pathetic creature who would so tear the heart from his breast and cast it before her haughty feet.

"Very well, Hector. You may endeavor to explain."

"Ah, lady, the history of my ailment—for that is the nature of my act—can be traced back to the days of my youth. A happy, carefree time it should have been, as it was for all of my fellows. After all, I was privileged, rich, not without charm, and although some said provocative, it was not so stated with malice. Cultivated to a fare-thee-well, I became proficient in the hunt, the arena of sport, and facile in four of the Romance languages. To the world I was Hector the Happy, envied, applauded, respected. Darling girl, believe me when I swear to you that it was for me nothing. I was then as I am now, the most unhappy as well as the most despicable of men. The reason? Well you might ask, although I know in what regard you shall hold me when the horrid knowledge is made yours. Tongue, speak on, or be swallowed forever."

"Hector," whispered Lavinia, speaking his name for the first time. "What? What in the name of God is it that you are saying?" Her white-gloved hand, which had, at the beginning of the meeting, clenched its mate upon her lap as though they two were a pair of Joans tied to a stake with the faggots aflame, stole furtively to her side, then, with a swift small pounce, landed lightly on his arm. Hector recoiled involuntarily.

"Lavinia, touch me not. I am tainted."

"Oh, my God, no." Her hand leapt back to huddle with its mate like a frightened child.

"Would it were no, but it is yes, yes, yes! The nature of my stain is . . . Strength now, Hector, courage . . . Mine is the spot of bastardy. Hear now, my dear; you've swooned. It's all right. There there. Come along. Where are your salts? Tucked in the waistband? Forgive me, lady, this fumbling for the vial. Here now, deepest draught. That's better." At the mention of the word Lavinia had felt her senses slipping and, in an effort to hold upright, had fallen across Hector's lap in the tenderest of sinkings. The hand that probed her waistband had hurled a net about her heart.

"Do go on, sir," she whispered at last. "I must hear all."

"I am not the son of the Duc de Savigny-Crespi. My father was a sometime shepherd from the Balkans, a Croat and an idler to boot. During a tour of those parts, he was in my mother's ken, if you will, for no longer than quarter of an hour. Of this you see I am the issue."

"And how, if I may ask, did you become aware of this?"

"My mother told the Duc one day while in a fit of pique over a quite imagined slight delivered at old Bucky during an audience with Her Royal. Fact is he had temporarily forgotten her name during an introduction. *Malheureusement,* I was secreted in the *portières* at the time and heard all. It is this dreadful knowledge that has colored my entire life, made a mockery of my ambitions, labeled me 'pretender' in the halls and rooms of Society, and blighted the hopes of every respectable person with whom I have been involved. You, Lavinia, are my last and greatest loss, the sublime object of the rage and destructiveness with which I strike back at life, at the world, at all decent men and women. It is this which compelled me to humiliate you on the eve of our betrothal. I could not marry you. I am not worthy. And now that you know, I shall take leave of you forever with only the tiny hope of your ultimate forgiveness to light my dark and sinister path. Good-bye."

"Ah, Hector, Hector," sobbed Lavinia, midway between laughter and tears. "How little you have understood me. Thirst explains me. And such a thirst as will ne'er be slaked save by the wine of you."

At this she rose from the bench and, voluminous in crinolines, turned to face the startled man gazing up at her. "And now it is I with a confession for you. I, too, am"—she searched for the word—"uniparental. No Croatian idler mine, but a butcher from Brighton. Hogs, if you please."

Hector rose to his feet, his body half crouching as though to receive a blow to the midlands. His eyes filled with tears and, shaking with fervor, he grasped her hand and bowed deeply, pressing the kidskin with his lips. Lavinia felt herself seized and dashed helplessly by giant waves of emotion.

"Our love shall wash away these sins, Lavinia. What is there that love cannot hallow? Let us share these secrets throughout our lifetime."

"Hector, my darling," she breathed.

"Lavinia," he exhaled.

In and Out

In

I shall lie on this bed for the foreseeable future. Remonstrances have no effect on me. I am resolved. Sometimes, if I keep my eyes closed, I dream that I am back there, swimming in the ruby gloom, suspended, effortless, thoroughly possessed and therefore loved. But they do not allow me even to dream. They come regularly with the feeding tube and syringe. Liquid nourishment is squirted into my stomach. They have become very adept at this ministration. I do not object, for it would be undignified. Three times a day I am wiped, bathed, and diapered. I take no notice. After all, I did not on my own initiate this chain of events. *He* did. Dr. Weiss.

"Ve shall go pack in time," he ordered. "Ve shall return to your childhood, vhere the puilding blocks of ze psyche"—he pronounced the silent *p*—"lie scattered in your blayroom."

How he fancied himself!

"It iss a long hard chourney, Mr. Schwartzkopf. Are you villing to make it?"

"Villing," I said.

And so we did. I am twenty-nine years old and it's a long way back. But as the months went by, step by step we retraced my serpentine path through life. At first it was tedious beyond description.

"Vy did you pretend to haff diarrhea ze night of ze high school chunior prom?"

"I don't remember."

"Tink back. Vas ze girl ogly?"

"No, not really."

"Vas she mean?"

I shook my head.

"Vas she stupid?"

Again I demurred.

"Zen vy? Vy? For Gott's sake, vy?"

"I don't remember," I said, bursting into tears of frustration.

"Dere, dere," soothed Dr. Weiss. "Don't cry. Ve shall go pack a little furder."

Six months later, imagine my astonishment to hear:

"Mr. Schwartzkopf! Take your tumb out of your mout!"

It was true! I was sucking my thumb. With what a rush of shame I whipped the offending digit from its warm nest and wiped it quickly on my trousers. I recall to this day the moist little noise that accompanied the extrication.

"Ve vill shtop at ziss point," said Dr. Weiss. "Ziss is far enough. Now ve shall pegin to reconstruct."

Easily said, but already I had begun to feel a subliminal current sweeping me along, a pull as though in the path of a tropism. Having stepped into the vessel and poled away from the shore, I was being carried down the dark narrow stream on demanding rapids, fending off the cliffs on either side; and at each turn in the passage I could feel new and subtle winds of discovery whisking around me. I had to go on. Do you understand? It was no longer a matter of choice.

How shall I tell all the ports of call, the harbors where flesh-toned towns glistened on hillsides that seemed to undulate in a warmth of their own making? I can but inform you of the ineffable joy, yes, radiance, in which I felt myself bathed, as each new station was realized. Suffice it to say that my journey was a perfect revisiting of the internal landscape, with the exception of one blemish, the eternal presence of that plague, that pest, that harpy Dr. Weiss, whose endless exhortation, rage, pleading for me to turn aside from my reconnoitering, to put aside (if you can believe it) my quest, would drive me to the heights of exasperation. At each turn I would look back over my shoulder, hoping to have escaped his baleful glower. Each time, what a flood of disappointment, even revulsion, as I saw him rushing up, his index finger a-waggle, his lips pumping in a constant slobbering harangue.

"Shtop, Schwartzkopf, shtop! I varn you, you go too far!"

At first I was outraged by his temerity, the sheer impudence of the man. How dare he attempt to sabotage me, to hurl himself in my path? And so I would call back:

"And *I* warn *you*, doctor, do not overstep yourself. I am in command here; not you nor all the gray eminences of Vienna and Switzerland can keep me from my quest."

I knew full well the reason for his insistence, the almost frantic measures he took to deter me, including—I blush to recall it—one occasion on which he leaped at me, a little trickle of saliva running from a corner of his mouth, and, gathering my neck scarf in the pudge of his fist, struck me again and again across the ears.

"Now vill you listen, you pad boy?" he screeched.

"Never," I said, with all the dignity at my command. "There is more here than thirty-five dollars an hour three times a week, sir."

Dr. Weiss was afraid. He could not hide it from me. Afraid that the monster he had created would turn upon him and wreak his own destruction. He was, if you will, looking out for his own skin, nor could I guarantee that he would be blameless, that he would not one day stand before a tribunal of his peers and hear the pronouncement of his own disgrace.

And then came the time when I was no longer to hear his

moist gargling. Alone and naked I stood before The Cavern. I could feel its humid vapors emanating, engulfing me, with their rich and beasty smell. I dared not gaze directly into the steamy recess, but averted my eyes toward the wise-looking gateposts, soft, tufted, and hung like the folds of some imperial drapery, such as must wind and billow about the waists of angels. What an impatience seized me! I found myself yearning for that cloudy passage, with all the—shall I say?—lust of the impending bridegroom. Exalted yet prostrate, I felt the slow sweet suction, the beckoning of the womb. Head bowed and arms folded upon my heart, I revolved into the warm membrane, turning, stretching, every part of my body hugged, snugly bound, drawn with all tenderness and love in and in, until I was *there.* What joy! I opened my eyes upon a world which was at once exotic and strangely remembered. Effortlessly I floated and turned in a liquid medium, folding one leg upon the other, waving my arms in a dance more sensuous, more lyrical, than any ballet. From far, far away I heard the last faint hoarseness of the doctor's voice:

"Schwartzkopf! Shtop!" and then no more.

Unburdened. To tell the truth, I would have been completely happy to remain in that state forever, endlessly toying with the mounds and spongy hillocks, nuzzling the compressible life-giving ridges. Yet even then I knew that this was not my destination, for almost at once there began the same restlessness, the same voiceless vocation toward a central core of enlightenment wherein all my mystery would be in an instant solved. What followed can best be described as a chaos of the tissues. It was as though all my flesh became molten, plastic. Ridges rose at one end of my body and rolled slowly across it to spend themselves into extinction at the other end. Suddenly fissures would open, cleaving me here and there, without pain or discomfort, I assure you, and all the while there was a migration of strands and sheets of cells, first in one direction, then in another, seem-

154

ingly without any purpose. But at each moment I was aware of a sense of simplification, a lessening of detail and complexity. I was less and less concerned with potential, with abilities, and more and more turned in upon myself, which was growing calmer, more serene, more stable, with each change. It was as though I were subject to the thumbprints of a potter, bent on smudging out the imperfections of a vessel.

That which had taken nine months to complete seemed to reverse itself within the space of days, like the rewind of a tape recorder. So hectic was the pace that it is impossible to recall what was synchronous, what chronologous. When did sight fade, dimming into night-heavenly black? When did the hands and feet group their digits, gently fusing them into soft hoofs, at first cloven, then solid? When did brain roll forward into a great frontal bulge, teeming with a billion unrealized thoughts? When in fact did the gill slits ride like chevrons on my neck? I cannot be specific in any way. Yet back through time from ape to pig to fish, riding backward on the steed of evolution to— what shall I call it?—Undifferentiation: a state more perfect, more complete, more sublime than any I had known. In time, I felt myself a whirling ball of cells, growing smaller with each revolution, a blastula, and utterly happy.

Falling away, deeper and deeper into the well of my past, intent only on pursuing to the end this odyssey, then out of control, I spun toward Unicellularity, bouncing deliciously among the billowy pink fronds, the purple gossamer membranes. Every sensory granule within me vibrated in excitement. Suddenly there was a sense of shearing, a fission, that to anyone who has not been so blissfully rent no description is possible. Suffice it to say that it is the sum total of all the sexual climaxes and moments of intellectual enlightenment of my life. At the end of that ecstatic ripping, I felt for the first time the sense of Duality. I was two! I had achieved the incredible. I had flung myself back in my past, careening down the corridors of

155

my years, and had entered the primal vale of Egghood and Spermhood. Now I was in a strange miasmal state, in twain: part of me heavy, globular, ample, sedentary; the other fierce, electric, motile. From Manhood to Egghood and Spermhood in one tumultuous headlong sweep. I can only describe it as the awareness that I was both here and there; in one, ripe, yolky, sessile; in the other, tailed, motile, a sinew. Back and forth from one half to my other I stared in resonating wonder.

Shortly I sensed a lessening of egghood, or rather a dominance of spermhood, as though the round fullness had drawn away and I was now magnetized, strong, brimming with energy, and leaping over the crested forefront of a swift current. At that moment I felt myself close to a profound truth, as though I stood at the threshold of a temple, more, before the Holy Ark whose golden curtain was even now parting to reveal the divine essence within. A wave of love swept over me. I could feel a powerful presence thrusting in upon me, pumping, a glistening dome of wisdom and force.

"Father!" I cried.

Now I understood everything, knew myself down to the smallest speck. I had gazed upon, felt, the very source, the fount, the mount of me, and if I sound a bit mad, it is because the impact of this knowledge stretched my consciousness to the very limits of containment and perhaps beyond.

Out

One glance was all, but in it all my truth. Then, pushed along in the surge, herd-spurting, compelled, aware of my strength, that I was the strongest, tireless, peripherally cognizant of my limp and flabby fellow-flagellants rocking belly-up in the backwash. I, oh, I! All fierce knob and whiptail, a jot of pure drive, swam on and up, breasting the current, never for an instant wavering in my search for that sublime quarry. There is no terrain so amiable as the Fallopian tube! No climate so salubrious as in that veiled tunnel whose slow undulation and gentle throb beget a satori-like detachment. What need have I for travel? What peak or valley, beach or plain would suffice? I have known the best of all landscapes. I should find all else banal in the comparing. That this was to be the chamber for my primal fusion, my fertilization, was eminently suitable.

I saw her, my bride, round as a peach and of the same delicate hue, perched among the velvet folds, her membranes throbbing with anticipation. And then the dance. Round and round the nubile sphere I swam, nudging her into a spin, at first slowly, then twirling faster and faster, feeling the quiver of her with each touch of my head. Like a moon she was, pale and virginal. Suddenly I could bear no more and with all my strength I lunged toward her. What sweet impingement, what delicious indentation. Thrust hard and sure until I felt I must die, totally sapped. At the last there was a give, and I leaped forward and through, feeling the yolky stuff envelop me, salving, warm, healing, fused.

As a blastomere I found life to be, in a word, ecstatic. Just imagine yourself a perfect little sphere, rocking gently to and fro, bathed all the time by the warmest juices, fanned by soft cilia, more luxuriant than the plumes of Cleopatra. And the cleavages—numberless and beautiful as the stars—as the whole welcomes the addition of each new and perfect cell. No need to hunt, kill, eat, discharge waste—even to locomote; just to be.

Of the rest I can recapitulate no more. It is enough to say that the implacability of development was upon me. There was no escape. I became a baby.

At last came my saddest hour. I was to leave. I was sunk in gloom, terrified of the separation. What should I have done?

Cast out in the cold where hard fingers would poke, and currents of air would sear my skin. Did I have to? I did not want to go.

"I'll stay here!" I cried. "I will! They can't make me. Those people out there don't understand. I need to be here. Maybe if I talk with them. Hey!" I called. "Out there!" I shouted. "Let me stay here, will you? If I come out you're going to have to take care of me. If I stay inside I don't need anybody. I'm all set. Come on. Hey, out there! Anyway, I'm not coming. I'll die here first. If you want me, you have to come and get me. Bullies! Bullies!"

Oh, God, it had started. The great pumpkinlike structure seemed to be seized suddenly by rough hands and pulled into an elongated squash. Then there was a grinding down.

"Aiee, my bones! Watch out! I don't want to go out there. I don't want your filthy outside," I called. I pressed my little red face into the spongy tufts and wept my heart out. Dejected. "I thought you loved me, Mother. Don't let them do it, I beg you. I'll be so good and quiet. I won't kick or stretch so willfully anymore. Please."

Again the battering ram is heaved to, and now my head is pushing down into the narrows. There is no room to turn. This organ, which minutes before had been my garden of delight, has turned on me in expulsion. Who would have thought it to have such a thrust, such strength and malice? Again and again my head is rammed against hard bony prominences and pressed there until it is no longer round but crushed and drawn out. All day the torture proceeds, never diminishing, always gaining in ferocity. At last my head is no longer free but wedged into a viselike canal. I am battered into motionlessness now, arms and legs limp and hanging, and still the relentless womb presses down, pushing against buttocks and feet. Here it comes, the final thrust. It is the greatest of them all. With my last bit of strength I reach blindly for the cord, the tube of life, with both hands. I have it! I hold on for dear life. Nothing will break my grip. Oh, God, those cruel lights, that air abrading my flesh, those clenching hands. I'm choking. I cannot breathe.

A finger is thrust in my throat. Is it possible? I am hung by my heels and beaten. All right, I'll come.

"Stop! Stop!" Horrified, I watch the severing of my cord.

"My cord, through which I have lived my entire life!"

It is a bereavement. I am alone, isolated as a fish in a well. I am wrapped and laid to rest. What's the use of crying? When they hand me into her arms my mother smiles and says, "My little son." It is beyond irony, it is beyond effrontery.

There it is. That is the reason I stay, folded upon myself, in this bed. I cannot go back again. Many times have I tried, to no avail. But I wait, always with the hope that I will feel the wind rise, the sails fill, the boards creak. Quick, hoist the anchor! We'll skim out to sea once again on the Great Adventure.

Oh, oh, here he comes. Dr. Weiss.

"Goot morgning, Valter." He has taken to calling me by my first name—a liberty which I find repugnant. "How iss my liddle baby poy today, eh? Going to talk to me, eh? Ve are friends, yes?"

No! It is all I can do to restrain myself from biting that chin-chucking finger. Yet that would cost me my state of readiness, so I do not. I content myself with a bit of judicious straining and a grunt or two. In a minute the session will be terminated. You'll see. I know him too well.

At the first grunt he calls for the nurse to change my diaper.

"Oh, nurse, vill you come, please?"

See, what did I tell you?

The Defense of
ibn-Biklarish

Listen! ibn-Biklarish is beginning the testimony in his defense.
How dignified he looks. Those eyes that have seen so much of
death and disease; what a melancholy flame burns there. I could
weep for him now. All in all he is a good master, and I regret
the days I have spent enjoying self-pity and complaining. And
that I have betrayed him, even I, Hajji, whom he plucked from
the bathhouse and made into an apprentice in his surgery. I had
seen him enter there and placed myself on view. He bathed
slowly, then sat alone smiling and braiding his beard. When I
drew near I could see that he was even then red-eyed with the
hashish which he had carried hidden in the sleeve of his caftan.
It is well known that passions are stirred by the weed and, truth
to tell, I was not unreceptive. He fumbled in his sleeve and
brought out a fulah of it, which he placed between my lips. I
ground it between my teeth and lay down to dream. Such an
innocent. He did not even know how to begin, but I helped him
along. So well that he wrote me three love letters in as many
days. To think that I sold them to his prosecutor for three pieces
of gold. Ah, shame on me and all of my forebears and descend-
ants. I am no more and no less than the shit of camels. But what
is a poor Arab boy to do? If I do not use the wiles and quickness
that Allah has given me, then am I not a fool—more, an ingrate
to God? Still, it was infamous of me to sell them. They were so

160

beautiful. "Most adorable waif," he wrote. "Divine boy whose cheeks are smooth and green as hashish. Persian antelope, how I love thy flanks and lids, thy sweet spittle, the plumshine of thine eyes, thine every part." And this in another: "Thou walking cypress, thou palm tree watered by a royal ditch, O thou whose buttocks are twin pomegranates hanging from a single stem."

Oh, heart, be still! Think of it no more. The pain of guilt is too griping to bear. All that keeps me from taking poison is the knowledge that he will forgive me. He did last night, in fact. He loves me still, you see. I had but to sob in his arms and hold myself against him, and all of his anger melted away. He told me that I am his disease, his fatal affliction, his necessity.

And now my beloved master is to be tried for that most reprehensible of crimes, malpractice. I need not tell you that ibn-Biklarish is the most famous and learned physician in all of Saragossa, nay, all of Moorish Spain. From his mortar and pestle have come the balms and salves to heal legions of believers and infidels alike. He is the reincarnation of the Persian sages, a holy man, a treasure of this world, but a Jew. In truth I do not hold it against him that he from Sarah while I from Hagar have sprung. It is the seed of Abraham that has fashioned us both. And it is well known among the Arab boys that Jews make the best masters. They are less perverse and more generous.

I knew at once that the villain Moustapha, brother-in-law to the Vizier, would bring my master nothing but harm. From that first moment when his decaying carcass was deposited in our hospital, I knew no good would come of it.

For weeks ibn-Biklarish has been preparing his defense. His lamp burns half the night, and page after page of barely legible writing lies strewn about his table. I very much fear he will grow ill himself, and then what will become of me? Oh, well, Allah will provide, and Hajji is not without things to sell.

If, in truth, it can be said that Nature reflects the deeds of men, there is reason to be more than a little alarmed. It is the day of the trial and dawn broke into the apothecary shop like a prowler, leaden-faced and grim. It is not a good sign that the sun is to hide itself from the events of this day. I myself rose early and worked feverishly among the patients and medicines in order to arrive at the court in time to hear the accusation.

I am embarked on a small pharmacological task of my own invention, unbeknownst to my master, although in due time I shall reveal all to him, that he may share in the riches and glory which I shall bring to his name. It is the concoction of a philter which I shall call Lover's Grass, a dirham of which, if applied to the genitalia, will produce blisters of such sublime irritation as to be irresistible to the frictions of love. Hitherto, my master has turned aside contemptuously from all such pursuits, deeming the entire subject beneath his dignity as a physician. Nevertheless, I, immodestly, have more insight and imagination in these matters than he, who is little more than a child. Thus do I act in secret to the best advantage of us both. The following is a list of the ingredients of Lover's Grass, the exact amounts and proportions of which the most ingenious of tortures would not extract from my lips:

root of long pepper, the pippali-mul of Sanskrit
seed of saltwort
white mangrove
dried carp gall (shabut)
dried partridge gall (qabaj)
oil of cantharides
Indian garden olive
peony (rose of the ass)
pistachio
soapwort
oleander

All the above are pulverized and kneaded with fresh sweet basil juice. The philter is to be administered to one with an empty heart. If taken by mouth, it may induce postcoital forget-fulness. With the omission of the cantharides, and molded into a paste with the sediment of old wine, it is excellent for rehard-ening the hymen if worn as a poultice all night.

But I have shamefully digressed. May Allah forgive me for dwelling overlong on my own interests at this, the hour of my beloved master's peril. As I have said, the crime of which he is accused is malpractice in the case of Moustapha, the brother-in-law of al-Musta-in, the Prince of Saragossa. The accusation states that this same Moustapha was delivered unto treatment by ibn-Biklarish for various severe ailments, during the course of which my master was said to be under the influence of hashish. It is also claimed that because of this and the resultant misman-agement of therapy, Moustapha was rendered permanently im-potent.

The courtrooms are crowded with the idle and curious. There is a festive air which to me is as frightening as the Pest itself. ibn-Biklarish is renowned and the case is scandalous, thus at-tracting much lewd interest. Alas, I have arrived too late to find a comfortable place of observation, and must stand behind a column at the rear. It is just as well not to be noticed by the members of the Vizier's household. At any rate I can hear per-fectly well, and can even get an occasional peek by bending around the pillar. The official accusation has already been read, and ibn-Biklarish has taken the stand. Listen:

"Excellency, it is known that the intention of the physician is to inquire into one's health, and his aim is to obtain it. He cannot do this except by the art of medicine, which is given as a gift of God. He who blames his physician discloses his ignorance; he is from the lowest class of people."

The crowd gasps! Such insolence! Such courage!

"Since it is from God that medicine is given, it is God that he blames. The physician is a servant of God and can bear no blame."

163

He speaks of God, always God, God this and God that, when everyone knows he is a Jew!

"Excellency, the nobility of each craft is determined by its subject (mawdu) and its purpose (ghayah). For example the shoemaker, whose subject is leather and whose purpose is shoes. Thus the mawdu of the physician is man, and his ghayah is health."

Oh, a telling point, a telling point, master. Speak on.

"Alas, the importance of the mawdu earns the physician more blame when he fails than gratefulness when he succeeds. Worm-eaten, knotty wood does not respond to the carpenter's craft. Unsuitable to the physician are the bald, the one-eyed, and those affected by the third kind of hectic fever."

Is he not the wisest of all men? I weep at his eloquence.

"I am charged by the ingrate Moustapha with having produced a permanent state of impotence because of having laid hands upon him while under the influence of hashish. So be it. Whatever the final decision of this court, they shall hear a recitation of the true facts and they are as follows.

"I first made the acquaintance of Moustapha in the month of Isfandarmudh when the moon was a pitcher of milk, pouring itself out in the sky. A more bloated skin of vinegar it has never been my ill luck to behold, all of his organs in an advanced stage of putrefaction from the excesses which he′ has enjoyed throughout his unbridled life. Mine eyes, accustomed to the grossest misshapings of the flesh, snapped shut at the first glimpse of that bag of a man bursting with rancid gases. But with the forbearance of the true physician, I welcomed him across my threshold, supported as he was by several low fellows in his employ. I should have turned him from my house without a word of advice, as would that perfumer ibn-Sulaiman."

Sulaiman! Physician to the Prince! *There* is an enemy made who will seek revenge.

"But I, Yunus ibn-Ishaq ibn-Biklarish al-Israili, forbearing in regard to faults, indulgent with people, erudite, humble, quick to goodness, and with great praise as being far from sin, virtuous and clean, inside and outside, welcomed him, as I say, to my dispensary."

Truth to tell, we have not always been so lofty. On a recent night, the master and I were awakened by the sound of moaning in the courtyard. ibn-Biklarish became furious. "The people grow more swinish each day," he grumbled, "inconsiderate of my rest and my need for solitude." Then he ordered me to send away the whole lot of them without so much as a single headache seed. "So much for braying within earshot," he said. "The spitting is poisonous. My rosebushes are spotted from it, and the blooms give off no scent but a sourness that clings to the clothing for days." As you can see, Biklarish has a certain flair for the decorative in his speech. May this stand him in good stead. Such gestures are not inexpensive. He loses much money in the way of fees. A day lost cannot be regained. And in any case, he did not sleep the rest of the night but lay awake tortured by remorse lest someone of the throng should die because of his harshness. I tried to comfort him with the thought that Allah knows best, and all of life is a painful seizure until one flops into the laps of the houris in Paradise. But he would have none of this, murmuring only that fame and greatness were a burden, and happy is he who remains ignorant and a pauper, for he is free of these weights and retains the glee of childhood.

"Once he was divested of his clothing and laid upon my table, I questioned him as to the history of his ailment. It seems that for the past twelve months he had noted the progressive swelling of the flesh of his legs until, at the time of his presentation, one could see that they were as sacs of water, which, when pressed with the examining fingers, remained pitted by the exact imprint of the fingers of my hand. Fits of weakness assailed him so profound as to send his brain sliding in his skull like the deck of a ship in a storm. At these times, he would fall

165

to the floor dribbling a wild foam from his lips, and loosing his water into his already poisonous raiment.

"Excellency, this was by all known standards a sick man. One whom it would demand all of my not inconsiderable armamentarium to cure. Taking up the challenge, I devoted myself with absolute singleness of purpose to the task.

"I palpated the sinew of his wrist there where the sages of Persia have taught, and where there is little flesh overlying to conceal its pulse. Four times it dragged like a scorpion, then leaped like a deer in the might of its lightness. By this alone I knew, as it is written, that the sorrows of death would soon encompass him.

"Between those massive waterlogged thighs lay in full swoon that famous Bedouin sheik whose wild charges and steely thrusts are said to have made invalids of three dozen women and half again as many boys. It is rumored that the mosaic tiles of his harem run red with the spatterings from his fierce copulations. Excellency, the man is maligned. A rabbit's foot was what hung there, so brown and matted as to suspect its having fallen ages ago into a vat of wine, only to have been discovered by some horrified drunkard at the bottom of his cup.

"My patient was the very embodiment of Failure to Thrive complicated by an unrelenting abuse of that receptacle of the soul which God in His munificence has given to each of us for His glorification. In short, Moustapha had totally, and without remission, flagged.

"It may seem to Your Excellency that I have dwelt overlong on the miserable clay from which I was, under pain of my own death as I now see, to reconstruct no less than a dashing prince. It would have been easier to make a necklace out of quicksilver. But I am a physician. No creature, no matter how loathsome or unpalatable to ordinary man, is outside the fence of my garden. Mustering all of my resolve, I proposed to lay hands upon and heal this man.

166

"Further historical remarks were made by the patient in a breathy little whine as though the sole passage for air lay high in the back of his nose, and none coming in the throat. Now and again his puffy hands would fight their way up into the air to pick at curtains and webs that he alone saw. He told me, in the most unpleasant complaint, of his impotence, which, with my life at stake, I have the courage to announce to this court has persisted for ten years. This despite all efforts to rouse the moribund toad. These details, which involve all manner of direct and indirect pulling, rubbing, licking, sucking, and tickling, I reject from this account as altogether disgusting and hateful. It is enough to say that the flute does not exist whose floating moan can coax this dead snake from its basket.

"From his body rose a wind as hot and moist as that which comes from the Negev. Enlisting the aid of my apprentices, I turned the patient on his side to examine the back. Upon separating the legs I would have been but moderately amazed to see a family of mice nesting among the encrustations of decay.

"So much for the history and the physical examination. The time had come to arrive at a name for the conglomeration of diseases. As is written by the sages, the most important part of the practice of medicine is the application of a name for a disease. This is more than half the distance toward effecting a happy outcome in management. The mention of the name, rather than striking fear into the physician, as well it may in the patient, is a source of comfort and reassurance and indicates that the matter lies well within the talent and ken of the doctor, who may then marshal his forces against the enemy.

"After a period of meditation, I determined that what was troubling Moustapha was none other than an internal eruption of the bile, so violent as to cause a serious imbalance between the yes and the no of the body, between its male and female, its white and its black. This overflow of the black bile must never be allowed to run unchecked in the body, for it is a snare and destructive to the whole of a man. As Asaf has written, the seat of reason is the brain, the seat of understanding is the heart, and fear and despair are in the dark places of the body where the black bile flows.

"Excellency, there follows an outline of the treatment given to the plaintiff Moustapha.

"*On the first day,* the patient was bathed over his entire body with wine, then rubbed dry with pumice. This alone deepened his color, bringing the blood to the surface. An enema of pomegranate juice produced excrement as black and scanty as a rat's. Root of mandragora was given to control the patient's incessant roaring.

"*On the second day,* the first letting was done. A new sharp fleam was selected, and the great vein of the groin entered without difficulty. After no more than two cups had spilled into the porringer, the patient fell abruptly into a desperate state. His skin became white as sand, and moist with a cold sweat of death. A dab of musk placed in one of his nostrils revived him and the bloodletting was discontinued for the day, although I am confident that it saved his life.

"*The third day* was reserved for cupping. This was done with eight hot glasses over the lower abdomen and thighs. Soon dark vapors were seen emanating from his flesh and beclouding the glasses.

"*On the fourth day,* a purgative was given and four suppositories of emblic myrobalan. The purpose being to cool the bile by bolstering the spleen, which stands on the left like a cold warrior, fighting the heat of the liver and its allies on the right.

"*On the fifth day,* I saw that the patient had not improved in any way, and in fact appeared to have grown progressively more stuporous. Therefore did I interrupt my ministrations, and seek to take counsel with my thoughts. Now two things that induce pensiveness in scholarly people are the cautious use of hashish, and the immersion of the body in hot and cold water alternately. Thus in the interests of my patient did I on the fifth day of treatment betake me to the bathhouse, concealing in the sleeve of my caftan a qurs of hashish. This I killed and ate upon my arrival. As Rhazi has written, hashish purifies the body as it enlightens the mind.

"Ah, the vagaries of Fate! Is there a man here who would condemn me were I not a physician, or had I taken hashish in a lovely garden where grayish pigeons coo by brooks? No. For that is enviable and romantic. Nor would one hesitate to kill me had I done so in a mosque. And as for the boy, one has but to study the legends of Arabia to see that al-Mounya himself ate hashish in a bathhouse and misbehaved with someone pretty. How many are there among the judges of Islam whose drink is the green one, who braid the hair of their beards, and rub antimony on their teeth to hide the vice?"

Yet take care, master, speak not overmuch about the weed nor, as Allah is in Heaven, about the bathhouse. I see the faces of the crowd grow oily with lewdness and the desire for your downfall.

"When was it that primitive man in pain writhing on some forest floor first crushed with his fist a clump of young unfolding ferns, and in his agony thrust the ball of fronds into his mouth, perhaps to keep from hearing his own screams? Within minutes a sense of peacefulness had come upon him, starting in his arms and legs, making them heavy and hard to move, and in fact there was no wish to move them away from the sweet relief of quietude. Surely this was the coming of death. Not at all. In fact, most delightful and, yes, pleasant. Thus do I, ibn-Biklarish of Saragossa, in the year 1109, envision the birth of medicine.

"Then he, my man of long ago, did not die, but fell into the deepest and most salubrious sleep, and rose in an ancient dawn renewed, and replenished as though touched by the hand of God. He stirred, first one painless leg and then the other, looked down at himself and saw, balled in his fist, the white tips of the fern, running still with a faint trickle of their juice. He smelled, licked at the drop that ran across his palm, and sank once more into a pleasant smiling slumber.

"How far have we come, indeed, from the charming self-experiment of this earliest of physicians, who, in a blinding light of inspiration, or dumbly, by the will of God, used himself as the object of scientific investigation. Yesterday alone I harvested twenty separate herbals from my own garden and have newly received an equal number of materia medica from the Persian ship unloading in the harbor. Of these I shall make drugs to restore health to all of Spain and the rest of the civilized world, until my name is enshrined forever in the illuminated manuscripts of medicine.

"Excellency, under the fikrah of hashish I have made many discoveries of benefit to the people. Forgive me the mention of one or two as examples. First, the cause of abortion, which is a wind in the uterus that I have called Ventosity of the Womb. The fetus, being small and weak, is easily carried away by a light wind. The treatment for this deadly breeze was also given to me in the pensiveness of hashish. An electuary is made in the following manner: words from the Quran are written on a paper: 'O God, Thou who has made the sky above, make this infant complete.' The text is washed off into a glass of water, sandalwood and oil of pearl are added, and it is given to the woman to drink."

He quotes from the Koran. Blasphemy. We are lost. The crowd murmurs against him.

"Now, the certain test for pregnancy. Place a fresh onion in the vagina at night. If the uterus is not blocked from the head by a fetus, the odor will appear on the woman's breath in the morning."

A point in our favor. See how they nod in admiration!

"The treatment of bastinado wounds."

Aie, a sore subject. I fear we may have need of this unguent before too long.

"Upon my return from the bathhouse, I entered the room where the miserable Moustapha lay wallowing. It occurred to me that he, too, might be helped to find relief by the very measures which I had taken in his behalf. Therefore I gave orders that strong hashish be killed and a tea concocted therefrom. The patient was then placed in a bath of hot wine and herbs, only his face being allowed to remain afloat and supported by my assistant. The hashish tea was then funneled into his throat until his great body grew limp and peaceful. He fell into a profound and restful sleep. From that moment the patient began to improve.

"*On the sixth day,* the yellow vanished from his eyes, and the swelling from his legs. His mind cleared, as was made evident by the return of a natural crankiness and petulance. For eight further days and nights this treatment was continued, each day revealing a nearer and nearer approach to full health. At the end of this period of time, which was the waxing of the moon or Ur-Bihishtmah, Moustapha at his own insistence was returned to his house carried in a chair. For these past three months I have heard nothing concerning the progress of Moustapha from himself nor anyone in his household. Nor have I received any payment for the services rendered him in all good faith. Nothing, I say, until six days ago, when I was approached by an officer of this court (whose bladder stones I have removed, may God forgive him) and handed the document of charges against me.

"Oh, day of infamy upon which I, Yunus ibn-Biklarish al-Israili, preeminent apothecary in all of Moorish Spain, beside whom all others are mere perfumers, am thus falsely accused, and forced before the court to defend my name. Such are the facts of this case. Let the court decide and act."

171

I am rendered faint with emotion. Perhaps I shall die of it here upon these official tiles. I must hold myself strong to stay and hear the verdict. What? Is there to be no time for thought or discussion? The judges have decided so quickly. It bodes ill. I know the predilection of the courts for excisional punishment. The eyes, fingers, testicles, penises, and tongues severed by the high and mighty would, if piled in a single place, mound pink and quivering to the sky. The judges remain in their seats to issue their decision to the court. Biklarish has risen to face them. His face is stern and lofty. He defies them!

"Three hundred strokes of the bastinado and thirty pieces of gold."

Did I hear aright? Allah be merciful. It is unjust. Three hundred strokes and thirty pieces, or was it thirty strokes and three hundred pieces? I am addled. "What was it, sir, did you hear?" The shame of it, the pain. What will he do? See how he remains unmoved by the announcement. He will give them no pleasure in it. Only I know how he is trembling in his heart. They lead him away to the yard. I must run to be near him.

Oh, my God, see how the brutes use him. He is to be punished tomorrow at dawn. Is there nothing I can do? My gold pieces! I have the three paid me for the letters, and two others that I have stolen from the apothecary shop. (God forgive me.) I shall take them to the scene of the beating. Perhaps a way will be found to the man who will deliver the blows.

I have not slept the entire night but have squatted upon my rug rocking back and forth like a madman, waiting for the morning. For hours I have struggled with the cruel demands of Fate. My gold, that was to keep me from starvation, and ugliness. But my master, whom I—yes!—love. I *do* love him. Ah, me, well do I weep.

The crowds have already gathered in the yard. I shall hover at the margins until the right moment. A commotion! There he is. They lead him by a chain around his waist. How grim his mien. I fear the shock will end his will to live. They have thrown him to the ground. His shoes are torn from him and his feet laid bare. His big toes are tied together and his legs swung up and over the bar. His hands are likewise bound at the wrist and swung to the bar. He hangs suspended. Aie! those poor dear feet. Now is the time for me to go to him. May Allah protect his poor servant.

"Who is it that draws near to the prisoner?"

"It is I, Hajji, servant and apprentice to Biklarish."

"Do not approach, fool. Keep yourself in the crowd, or fear for your life."

"Surely you will permit me to bathe the face of my master, and to offer him a single sip of water. Lest he die."

"Take that for your daring, rogue, and that and that."

"Aie, aie." The blows are hard and bitter. I must weep, for I have not Biklarish's courage.

Still, I open my palm and flash the gold, once and quickly, but he has seen.

"What is it that you want here, knave? The guards will kill you. Begone."

"One sip of water for my master. Three pieces of gold for you."

He pauses. Greed brightens his eyes with the reflection of my gold.

"Quickly then. No more than an instant, or you die."

"And two more pieces if you miss every other stroke, only pretend."

He is huge and ugly with an underlip as moist and drooping as that of a camel.

"Softly, scum." The hissing in his voice tells me that he agrees.

I run to the prisoner, cradling his head in my lap.

"Hajji, Hajji, my love." His voice is broken with the emotion of seeing me here. He weeps for the first time.

173

"Take these in your mouth, master. You shall not mind the whipping," and I thrust two dates between his lips, dates that I myself have stuffed, one with opium, the other with hashish.

Even though it pains me beyond any telling, I must stand in the forefront of the throng, and watch the beating, so that the brute will not betray me. There it is! The stick! The dreaded bastinado! Three hundred to the soles of his feet! But a hundred and fifty if I have succeeded, and the drugs, the drugs will spare him. They must! See, he is as though sleeping, a faint smile upon his face. The first blow has fallen with a horrid slapping sound. But ibn-Biklarish lies still. It is good. It is good. I have saved him. And yes, he *does* miss every second stroke. Curses! I shall have to pay him, the villain, the good villain. Alas, my only gold.

It is done. The men untie him. They will leave him to me now.

"Here is your gold, man. May Allah give you further reward."

"Come, come, master, I shall carry you home. Climb upon my back. Aie! those bleeding feet. When we get home, Hajji will bathe them and apply poultices of the very unguents that you have devised for bastinado wounds of the feet. Last night I mixed and ground the herbs and it is fresh and soothing. Do not cry so, master. It is disheartening to me. Come home, and I shall treat you as my little baby, and then we will play, just we two, as much as you want. I have a philter that will surprise you."

Midnight Rising

Autumn. Riding through a stained-glass country. The colors become more and more daring, outrageous, then lose control completely. That wall, the great lawn. The gate. Did ever one . . . ? Black, it clangs, and I am Within. The apertures of the grille are so small that a child's hand could not pass. To have left, and never to go back! The hall has widened. It is boundless and light and the antechamber recedes into dark narrowness.

From the first, I love this coolness and shadow, the absence of sound. This convent is my world, my home. I follow the nun down a long corridor, at the center of which she stops. Another nun is kneeling before a small statue of the Virgin, rosary in her fingers, her lips in a ceaseless murmuring. We move on. The Sister speaks.

"We have undertaken to carry out Perpetual Adoration of the Virgin here, in addition to our other Divine tasks. The choir nuns take turns by the Virgin, sending a constant stream of prayer to her. We do not wish her to be unattended for a moment."

There is a faint smell in the convent. What is it? I cannot place it. A cool smell, as of ashes or honey or wine. I am never to be without that odor again. It will cling like an essential vapor as I move through this cloister. I am led to my cell on the second floor, one of many small rooms opening on a rectangular hall, the center of which is a broad stairwell. There is a heavy oak

175

door with a central square of open latticework through which observations can be made. This barren cell of stone and wood.

"Our life is plain, you see."

"Yes."

The nun leaves with the instruction to change into the habit that lies upon the narrow bed. The white wool has a clean, rough feel. I slip off my outer clothing and get into the habit, which is put on over the head. It falls to the floor, just the right length, as though I, specifically I, have been expected. Above me on the wall, gleaming arms ripple apart to spiked palms, and the punctured side quivers in a spicule of sunlight.

There is the tapping of a stick upon the lattice. I step into the hall, and in the gloom see the pale cloud of nuns float silently toward the stairwell that leads to the choir. I am part of the cloud and stand at my place in the choir. The chanting begins. From the very beginning, I feel a warmth rising in my body. I am imperturbable. There is a glee in me. The next day, Reverend Mother breaks her silence.

"We live in the antechamber of Heaven. For that we must always be ready, on call as it were. A summons to prayer is one of immediacy. It is an urgent call. Rise from your bed and hurry to the choir. God hungers for prayer. Feed Him." I see the soft folds of her face tightening with verve.

This idea of alertness had not occurred to me. I had envisioned a life of slow rhythms and quiet exultation. But now I am to lie in my bed at night with the anticipation of prayer upon me and leap to the sustenance of my Saviour. For twenty years, at midnight, I am to stand in the choir to sing the Divine Office. I have always felt most fully alive at midnight. I can remember waking as a child to hear the twelve strokes, waiting for each one, not daring to breathe, lest they stop short, lest there be but eleven, or ten. And feeling, even then, an exhilaration, a danger. At midnight I am open and unlimited.

There was to come a night when I could not sleep, when I

waited for the Midnight Rising with my heart beating rapidly, disciplining my body to lie still. I have always awakened some minutes before the call and waited for the tapping on the wooden grille of the door. That night I listened for a premonitory sound, the coursing of a woolen habit through the corridor, the earnest breath of the caller. No sound. I listened in the hush, for what? A flutter of wings? Could it be? The possibility blazed before me. At the sound of a stick upon the grating, I rose and was immediately at the door. I slept fully clothed, as did the others. It is part of the state of readiness which prevails at the convent. The choir and the chanting had begun. I trembled. There was an uncontrollable need to smile, a quickening of my breath and pulse. I was seized and dashed against rocks. There was pain and joy. I could not distinguish one from the other. As the voices died, I sank to my knees, spent, able only to pray:

"O Jesus, my heart."

Reverend Mother has been here with me for eighteen years. Her kindness has enveloped me, infinitely comfortable, body temperature, membranous.

I cannot keep from smiling. At times I feel that I ought to repress the laughter within me, to discipline my face, and yet I cannot. I am too happy. I submit eagerly to the fasting, the abstinence from meat, the silence, the paucity of water (a single pitcher a day for bathing), to all the impositions of the Order. Of all, I find it easiest to empty my mind of thought, save that of God. For me this is no task, requires no discipline. I need no alternate idea. . . .

For some weeks, I have felt an uneasiness. My nightly ecstasies have become apparent to the others. Last night, there was a tremulous slowing of the chant as I experienced again the exteriorization of my soul. They are aware, I well know, although for months there has been no overt acknowledgment.

Today, I have been Proclaimed!

"I must now Proclaim Sister Mary Michael, who in an unseemly and ostentatious manner disturbs the midnight prayers. She is given to loud breathing, moaning, and whispering outside the text."

What is said at Proclamation is intended to air grievances, bring faults to light, that the community may function in a more perfect unison of spirit and that the offender may humbly accept the criticism of her Sisters and strive for control of her fault. I cannot stop shuddering. I feel discovered, shamed by the accusation, yet, even as I bowed my head at Proclamation, the anticipation of Midnight crept over me and I knew that in this one matter, I could not and would not submit. To restrain, hold back, dam up? No, it is not possible. It is to ask me to imprison my soul when He beckons it from me. Indeed, I have long felt myself apart from this community. The furies and spendings which are mine alone I have never shared with the others.

Danger!

This house is infested. The lice of envy hop and creep upon the cold skins of my Sisters. In rage they scratch at themselves. Soon they will scratch at me. I am fully cognizant of the race for sanctification that exists here, hard-fought and desperate. No more do I see smiles, the soft bustle of cloister life. Refections, taken always in absolute silence, are scenes of cold isolation. The impulses I feel from my Sisters are silently expressed and silently experienced; nonetheless, they are exquisitely barbed and most directly aimed. The subdued clatter of tin utensils is singularly absent at my end of the long refectory table, as though to join in a mutual hubbub would signify a sense of amicability toward me.

I am walking in the corridor and pass the Reverend Mother's office. A delegation of visiting priests is seated therein and, not quite out of earshot, I hear my name.

"Sister Mary Michael has been with us eighteen years, Fathers."

I pause in the passageway, listening.

178

"From the moment she arrived, I was aware of the difference in her, the heightened sensitivity. The possibilities in her case have long been known to me."

So! Reverend Mother knows of my passions, knows and hopes for my special significance. I retreat to my cell and fall upon the bed, exuberant, wild. I wait for the Midnight Rising with an unendurable feverishness and impatience. Twenty times I rise from the bed to stand rigid in the cell, feeling the muscles of my body taut, the cold dampness of my hands. Each time I return to my bed, unable to loosen the constriction which makes me twist upon the mattress as though seeking air to breathe. The stick upon my door! Up and into the hall, rushing down the stairwell to my place in the choir. I hold myself tightly in until the others are in place and the recitation has begun. At the first pale sounds, I give way and a sob escapes from my throat. A momentary hesitation from the choir, then the chanting resumes. I yield to the spiritual penetration that comes with unheralded intensity. There is no means of releasing the pressure of the inexpressible. At the end I kneel, leaning my head on the lectern, unrecovered, unaware that the others have withdrawn from the room.

Reverend Mother is leaving! My God, the others hate me so. For the first time, I feel panic. Mother has announced this morning that she is being transferred—Kenya—to establish an African convent. She has not sought me out for any special message but rather made a general statement to the Sisterhood. I must go with her, I cannot stay without her, it is impossible to stay. I have lost everything. O my God, will you perceive me if I am not here? In the same way, each night? Dare I ask to go? Is it this ground, this cell, this choir, that is the only chamber for my devotion? Would it leave me in another room, another garden? I am used to these paths only. No, I cannot go. For here I know Divine Love and the rest does not, must not, matter. O God, help me!

The nuns have bade Reverend Mother farewell. I alone remain with her.

"You must eat and rest more, Sister Mary Michael. Your cheeks are like ivory."

It is not food nor rest that I crave. I need more Midnight. I watch her disappear through the gates. How do I guard myself? I must make myself sly for Him. With what a furious fear I wait tonight for midnight. Would He come? I wait, and twist myself. He comes! He comes and the sense is greater. Oh, delectable embrace—this passing over, this flowing away, this sinking down. Tonight He holds out the red heart from His body to me and I strain myself upward to offer my own breast in return. I cannot live much more in this intensity. Yet I cannot live at all without it.

Her successor has been named. I am lost. Of all, she is the most implacable. The most gifted hater. I have seen her face grow grim and hard when she is near me. There is nothing between us but rancor. Heaven knows I bear her no malice.

"Sister Mary Michael, I have summoned you for a grave purpose. I have long been disturbed by your nightly performances. Far from a sign of saintliness, it is a manifestation of your own selfishness. You have always willfully set yourself against the congregation and striven for individual holiness. The Sisterhood is troubled. Sentiments of antagonism and outrage are in every corner of the Cloister. Your behavior must be controlled, or I shall deny your presence at the Chants."

Deny my presence! And yet I must pursue to catastrophe the course I have followed. I have thrown myself into the unfathomable and, stone that I am, must sink forever in a sea without bottom.

Again the Midnight ardor. And now no more. I have been forbidden to take part in the night prayers. What a cruel convent this is! Oh, this hatred that I feel—it bubbles out of my mouth. I walk the marble floors like a sick witch. I cannot keep from staring. I cannot blink my eyes. The food disgusts me, and I do not, cannot, pray. I have no word for my bereavement. I awake in the night with spittle on my pillow. How can I live? Today at the Mass, I felt a great nausea and weakness. They say that I fainted, and I awoke to the forcing of drink upon me. Later, the Reverend Mother speaks:

"Sister Mary Michael, the excitement of the Sacraments is too much for you. Your nervous state is apparent to all. You shall not attend the Mass until further notice."

Not attend Mass! To take away the Sacraments from a Religious! What is there left? But I have already lost much more. My Dearest and Best.

What tension strains through these rooms! I am being watched at all times. One further error and I shall be lost. What can they do to me? I must be careful, careful, careful. I have learned to control my breathing. I exhale very softly and slowly, and inhale in the same way, never too deeply, lest some sound escape and be heard. Material is being gathered to present to the priests. Each sound, each glance, is recorded to my devilment. I have not looked at anything in weeks. It is not, as they think, a distraction; it is cold power of my will. I keep my gaze ahead of me at all times save in the privacy of my cell. A single glance will be misinterpreted. Do I have the strength for this? I long to weep. Such a luxury I cannot afford. Or howl.

One night I awoke to hear the sound of laughter. It stopped the instant I leaped from the bed, but the echo, I swear it, the echo still flowed in the room. I knew in a second that it was my own laughter. In a dream I had been reinstated. I was returning to the choir, and a joy burst from me. Had I been heard? In the black stillness? I crouched in a corner on the floor. No sound. I leaned upon the thick darkness; it supported me and I remained there until dawn. The morning call, and I was found still leaning, but the darkness, my strut, my prop, was gone and I fell forward. I was taken by nuns, seized and held in their strong hands. I saw them hard and smiling, the bones of their fierce faces bursting through the dry skin.

"Sister Mary Michael, you must leave the convent. If you stay, you will be ill for the rest of your life. You will be better off in the world."

These clothes disgust me. The car has arrived and Reverend Mother is walking with me to the gate. In a minute I shall pass through into the world. It has been twenty years. Will I be able to breathe? Perhaps I am as ill equipped for that as a fish in the air. And as just such a fish twists, shiny on the leaves of land, throbbing open his gills wider and wider to find the water he needs, so do I. There is the gate! It clangs and I look back through the bars, I, who have fused with the substance of my Divine Cage. Like a wild beast freed from his cage of twenty years, who lopes off sideways toward the hated world, one glance smoldering back to his nest. Then turns to spend himself upon the impossible city.

Of my exile, only this. I shall call it my Want. The noise, the terror, the submerging of all into a kind of hollow . . . what is the use? I feel again the bite of monsters who leap from beyond the crags of wild landscapes. And the thousand dark nights of Yearn. For the White Stag upon the hill. That was my real life. What I do outside is to move toward death with the measured tread of the outcast. Shall I tell the low hours?

I live in a room. A college is nearby, and I rise prayerless. Tunneled into an ungainly costume, I shy along the pavement. There is an office, a desk, cabinets, and people who write, index, file. I write, index, and file, too, then slip away through many doors to sit upon my bed in the gloom.

My employer comes to my desk. "Marie, I want you to take this radio. I have no use for it, and it will while away the evenings."

One night I turn it on and hear the voice. It is harsh, reproachful.

"Sister Mary Michael, stand up." I stand up. "I have been calling you. Why do you not answer me? Hear me! Soon it will be midnight. Hurry!"

I can hardly breathe. Fear draws my hand to my mouth. Fear sinks my teeth in the soft skin and draws blood. I have to run, to leave, to find . . . I do not know. The night is cold and I run through the fog. When? When? Now? Please now? A star shimmers brilliant through the haze, becomes larger. It is descending upon me. Wait, stop! It has come for me. It seizes with an ugly thudding sound. And I lie upon the street.

"My God, I didn't see her. She was standing in the middle of the road. Call an ambulance. Are you all right?"

The dark.

The wound is in my right side, below the ribs. From the very first I am made aware of its presence by a faint odor, not unsweet. I have nothing to compare it with, perhaps a gardenia far away. Is it pain? Yes, but something else, too. A hot pleasurable sensation which relieves. There is movement in it, as though a worm coils and uncoils in its depth. It both pains and pleases. For many weeks I have lain in the hospital. An expectancy is upon me. I am waiting for something, but know not what. The doctors have told me that I had been most seriously injured, a crushing injury to the pancreas, they said. There had been an emergency operation. I had recovered and here upon my side is the sole residual of that night, this wound.

My wound! I love to watch them change the dressing. It is always the same. The red lips, strong, the gleaming scarlet cliffs, diving deep into my center. The slow trickle of faint pink liquid which wells from one corner and weeps across my flesh. And always the stirring that I feel at its base. . . .

A priest comes. I am to return to the convent! There is no

place for me in the world. I need care. He has arranged for me to go back if I would. If I would! I know at once that it is the wound. He talks of facilities and nurses and transporation and support. And I know it is the wound. I see his face when he inhales the odor. He cannot hide from me his wild acknowledgment. I am going back!

At last! The clanging of the gate was a peal of joy. The soft white wool is upon me and I lie in my cell until it is time. Gentle nuns dress my wound and take upon their fingers the warm extrusion. I see in their eyes an awe. At midnight I am led to the choir. I stand, a silver goblet brimming with wine. Sip, sip, Jesus. Sip. I feel the squirming life in my side. It grows warmer and I cannot resist. I have within me the White Stag's heart and oh, how it thrills.

Myself Healed

I would make my own diagnosis. Without the aid of—no, in very spite of those miscreant doctors, stupid men who warm their arrogant fingers in the orifices of their unwary patients. Who knows what perverse, bestial thoughts oil about in their mean brains? And, ah, their eyes, cynical and professionally glum, that fend off good news with expressions of outrage and ill-concealed avarice.

For months they have prodded my armpits, spread apart the buttocks to peer into my rectum, palpated my liver and spleen until these poor parts are bruised and softened. Like dogs they have cocked an ear to the soft noises of my body, the beating of my heart, the soughing of my breath, the borborygmi of my intestine. My fluids and my solids have they drawn off and collected in containers, each portion sniffed, smeared, strained, and stained. Little chunks of my flesh have they chipped away, these cut into fine slices and embedded in wax to be examined under the microscope. Me! Trapped in paraffin and scraped like a carrot. My flesh that God created in his image! There are twenty-four hour specimens of me, great jars of bile and gastric juice, cartons of stool, flagons of urine, and endless tubes of blood. Even the sweat has been scraped from my skin to be funneled into tiny Ehrlenmeyer flasks. My very marrow has been sucked up and smeared upon countless glass slides that they might study the arrangement of its cells as though in the

cryptic message of their pattern lay the secrets of enlightenment.

Let me delay no longer to tell you what it is that "ails" me.
A plant grows inside me. Yes, that is correct. Do not, I pray you,
adopt that arch-browed, mouth-pursed look as if to say, "Be
careful, he is mad." Nor dare to be indulgent. No, I tell you with
the firmest sort of assurance that there is a plant within me. A
vine, dark and sturdy, whose muscled tendrils even now grapple the coils of my intestine. I have been clenched by it much
as Laocoön and sons by their external constrictors.

I tried to tell them. Listen, I said, it explains so many things:
the gradual sense of tightening that I have experienced, starting
at the navel and radiating therefrom to the lower rib cage; the
greenish cast to my skin as the creeper smears its toxins on the
membranes. But they shrugged, and rocked back and forth on
their heels, and gazed out the window. In the end, I gave it up.

From the beginning I have known that it is a vine. When I
close my eyes and gaze inward, as I have taught myself to do,
I see pointed holly leaves atop long hairy stems. Its exact
nomenclature escapes me, as my knowledge of botany is rudi-
mentary at best. Nevertheless I know in my heart it is a vine.
I should have resented less a fern, I think. I am partial to them,
and surely it would have been less abrasive, less binding. I could
have come to grips earlier with a fern, à la Jonah and the Whale.
The young frondlets are especially lovable, rising from the
trunk like little clenched fists which open delicately to scatter
their leaves about them. Even an African violet would have
been better. Margaret used to grow them, called them her
"candied darlings." I have always hated them—hundreds of
small blooms, all shades of purple, and no distinction whatso-
ever. They had names like "Rob Roy" and "Ballerina."
Nonetheless I would have given all in all to have one of those
dainties within me instead of this ropy squid of a vine. Then

again, maybe not. I should be exchanging pain for nausea in that case.

So much for diagnosis. Now therapy. How to get rid of it before it sopped from me the last drop of succus entericus, and with it my life. I knew that I must remain calm, but such ideas as the following agitated me to the point of frenzy. Were the roots to push caudad, thought I, and the trunk thrust ever cephalad, should I not at last have a moment of possibility? i.e., that moment when the root were to present itself at the anus. At such time, should I not be able to seize it with my hand and, wrenching downward, secure that wicked ball to the out-of-doors? Cut it off with a knife or a pair of pruning shears? I had no evidence that such was its growth habit. For all I knew, the root was happily embedded in the steamy recesses of my caecum, and with no proclivity to migration. Yet we follow such wild quests, do we not, with the zeal and singleness of purpose of compulsive madmen?

Therefore did I place myself supine upon the floor of my bedroom, with my legs elevated until they swung above my head, overhanging the shoulders in the so-called exaggerated lithotomy position, that most vulnerable of attitudes. With the aid of an elaborate little system of mirrors, I was able to bring into focus that very part through which I envisioned the divine extrusion, if you will permit me one sad little jest. In this wise, for hours, with the concentration of a Zen priest did I peer— no, study the aperture whose every pucker and crease were to become as well known to me as the terra cognita of my hand. Indeed, I begrudged the blinking of my eyes lest it rob me of the first telltale sprout of a rhizome. Only when my neck and shoulders could no longer sustain the burden of the lower half of my body, only then would I tear my gaze from that portal and slowly, painfully, lower my hips, knees, then feet, to lie there exhausted, yet already regrouping, gathering my strength for

187

the next watch. Of my accouchement . . . for it was midwifery that I practiced there upon the floor next to my bed, and deliverance that I sought.

Alas, no single dendrite did I espy.

Conversely, I have stood before the bathroom mirror and with equal intensity stared into my pharynx, as though by the very force of my will I could coax the ultimate apical leaflet to flutter into view between the tonsillar pillars. No gardener greedy for the first genetic glimpse of green after the endless winter matched me in my hunger for the first sighting of my parasite. But no. The skulking predator adventured not forth. Then hatred consumed me for the creature marauding from within what it feared to grapple face to face.

At one point, driven by failure and frustration, I sought consultation with an herbalist, Hecanthra by name, a sour-smelling old woman who spent her days grinding the dried pods she would gather from the forest floor. She insisted first that I undress, then, while I stifled my revulsion as best I could, she stroked my abdomen with her dry, cornified fingers, beneath whose nails I envisioned the crushed corpselets of worms and nameless subpetrous insects collected in her incessant scrabbling.

She leaned forward to sniff my navel, pressing the prong of her beak to my flesh as she did so, and all the while her edentulous gums swiveled against each other in a kind of continuous self-abuse. At last, she drew off to one side and squatted on her haunches, where she remained for the better part of an hour. When she returned to me she was holding a greased milkweed pod stuffed with God knew what horrid medicaments. This she used upon my person as a suppository, with I leave it to you what shame and discomfort on my part. In addition, she bade me drink a vinegar sauce which she swore would shrivel an oak tree. Suffice it to say that aside from a disastrous bloody flux, my condition remained unchanged.

I had thought my case to be unique in the annals of medicine. (I persist in referring to my "duality" as a disease only in the interests of simplification and readability.) Actually, I was coming more and more to the realization that it is indeed something else, an extraordinary mutation, if you will, a rare example of the unification in one organism of the plant and animal kingdoms, which, in my humble opinion, is the direction that evolution will take within the next few thousand years. I am but the forerunner, the herald, of a whole race of what I have tentatively entitled "Planimals," thinking the corollary "Aniplants" lacking somewhat in seriousness of tone. . . . Again, in the beginning I was under the impression that I was unique, the sole example of an unusual form of parasitism, or, as much time elapsed and I became aware of the essential benignity of the host-growth relationship, saprophytism. Since then, my studies in the archives of surgery have brought to light two other cases of this phenomenon. One, a man in Tierra del Fuego who astonished his surgeon by presenting him with an appendix inflamed by the presence of a germinating seed in its lumen. That surgeon proved his unworthiness by throwing away the seed and with it all possibility to pursue the nature of the throw-ahead which I choose to call now "Florafaunism." Instead, he maundered on in the scientific literature about the vagaries of appendicitis, and the fate of ingested foreign bodies. As I read his irrelevant report in the *Proceedings of the Society of Chilean Medicine*, Vol. 14, No. 22, I was seized with such a sense of outrage that I inadvertently cried out, "The seed, fool, the seed. Did you not plant it?"

Somewhat less scientific, but certainly richer in style, is the second case, that of Signora Theresa di Stefano of Gallipoli, a desiccated village of southern Italy, who with her husband, Luigi, tended grape arbors from which they extracted each autumn a particularly rancid zinfandel. Whether one attributes it to the inheritance of acquired characteristics, or to some as yet unclarified form of toxicity, it is known and documented that the children of this couple—one male, Giangiacomo, and one female, Felicia—were born with a rich purple color to their skin, and almost from infancy complained of peculiar identical griping pains radiating from their navels. The entire matter would have lain dormant had it not been for the insinuation of a cruel and sly Fate which ordained that Felicia, upon her twelfth birthday, should become pregnant by the libertine tenor of a traveling opera company, and nine months later should spontaneously deliver herself of clusters of luscious dark grapes of a bouquet unmatched for its beauty in the entire Italian peninsula. This occurrence was absorbed by the community and her family as a miraculous announcement of forgiveness by the Virgin Mary, and a restoration both symbolic and actual of the virginity of the girl. Accordingly, Felicia's mother, Theresa, in an act of truly touching adoration, concocted a wine from the newborn grapes which is still used each year in the Festival of the Virgin Mother. Naturally, one might be skeptical of the aura of folk and place which has surrounded this event, but the central biological facts are undeniable, having been attested to by a papal nuncio and a group of hostile Southern Baptists, among others.

Admittedly these two cases do not possess the neat click of a laboratory switch. Still, even the most starch-collared anthropologist would hesitate to give the lie to our most colorful myths; take, for example—to remain in Italy for a moment—the one concerning Romulus and Remus, suckled by a wolf, or the notorious Rape of the Sabine Women, about which happenings there is not a jot of evidence, but the very tenacity with which they have clung to the hills of Rome, imparting their special fragrance to the history of that city, lends them more than credence. The truth survives. If one does not believe that, then one has lost all hope for mankind, and one is a swine. I myself have come to look upon this second case, the incident of the Virgin Grapes, as a kind of religious allegory from which moral truths can be drawn.

I suppose I should have told Margaret about my condition before we were married, but truly, I was scarcely aware of it myself at that time, and had experienced only the first faint intimations of Florafaunism. It is even possible that my pale green complexion, and my habit of pressing both palms to the sides of the rib cage to still the fluttering within, lent me a certain air of "romance," *une belle différence,* if I may, that was attractive to her. Somewhat slight of build as I am, although muscled and strong, I assure you, these two eccentricities gave a poetic ambience to my carriage. In any case, I know now that I was for her something to be nurtured, cultivated like one of her damned African violets. There were even times when I could have sworn that the same fish meal with which she fed her "darlings" was strewn upon my salad. Her nickname for me is, in retrospect, quite revealing. I was to her "Little Prince Greentease," a perfect name for an anemic violet. It must be said, however, that under her fluorescent vigil I bloomed, took on bulk and stature, waxed, despite the persistence, in truth deepening, of my greenishness, a fact which did not appear to upset Margaret at all. Did I, unconsciously, choose for my wife a gardener of plants, knowing on some elemental level that she was necessary for my survival? Was this marriage which ended in Hell actually made in Heaven? To this day I wonder.

When I announced to Margaret that I was through, leaving, fed up with a relationship which had diminished to the level of a daily watering, she expressed no obvious regret or surprise. Perhaps there was just the slightest emphasis to the way she broke off a leaf pocked with brown spot from her prize-winning double-frilled "April Showers" as she nodded in agreement. But after all, she is only human. Some sign of acknowledgment of our eight years together was not unexpected. The next day I had left, and since then have devoted my life to the understanding of my condition.

It must now be said that within the past six months I have entered upon a new phase in my study of this matter. There came a time when I stopped struggling to rid myself of the vine, to expel it through one or another of my orifices. I suppose that I simply grew tired. It takes stamina to sustain such an effort, and, in the end, mine ran out. I took to my bed, and lay there listening as to a ticking clock to the cellular multiplication taking place within me, the mitoses that would one day soon, I thought, encroach upon me in some vital way, and destroy me. It was a state of sad expectation such as is seen in the men of a garrison long under siege, who, at last, starving, out of ammunition, bled out, have hoisted the flag of surrender, and now wait and listen for the marching feet of their conquerors. So did I lie in wait, vacant, and resigned.

I cannot recall the precise moment when the idea occurred to me. It was as abrupt as a shaft of grace. But that is of little importance. What does matter is that quite suddenly I knew that my vaunted desire to devine myself was an artificial construction on my part. Into the void that was my mind crept the realization that the vine had become the very architecture, the framework, and lattice upon which my flesh was strung. Take it away and I would fold, slump, run down, spineless and devoid of fiber. By some opacification of insight I had overlooked the beating heart of the matter, the essence of it, and that is the absolute need that the plant and I had for each other. Suddenly I asked myself what I would be without it, what would be my concerns, where my devotion directed, and the answer was as death-dealing to me as would be the rupture of the root from its stem. In short, we were and are necessary to each other. There is between us a need that is more than mere dependence, more than the fact that we feed upon each other, clear each others' wastes, shelter, brood, nest, conceal, comfort, and accompany each other. In short, to give it a name, it is love. Yes, love, and a kind of love such as I have never known, a privileged, rare love that recognizes its ecological completeness, and accepts it ungrudgingly, that sees its evolutionary destiny with courage. Such a love knows nothing of jealousy, or fear of inadequacy, or comparative performance.

With this realization came also my well-being. Insight has cured me, not of a disease, but of the failure to recognize my great good health. No longer do I feel the old griping pains, but rather a gentle internal massage which is expertly delivered and utterly fulfilling. No more the anxious examination of my skin, hoping for an ebbing of my color. I am proud to be a member of the green race. Let those who mock me scurry among the crags and swamps of this uncomfortable planet, hissing with need. *I* am well.